THE KISS KEEPER

KRISTA SANDOR

CANDY CASTLE BOOKS

This book is dedicated to bug juice, sailboats, campfires, first kisses, and endless summer days.

FREE 15-MINUTE QUICK-READ ROMANCE

LIP LOCK LOVE-A STEAMY SHORT STORY

A crash course in kissing can't be that bad? Or can it? *Lip Lock Love is a steamy short with all the feels.* Use the link to get your ebook: https://BookHip.com/BAPLQQ

PROLOGUE

"Natalie, we know you're not asleep. Stop stalling and get down here!"

"Yeah, what Les said! We know you're awake, Nat. We can hear you breathing," her cousin Lara chimed, always piggy-backing off Leslie and never the sharpest knife in the drawer.

Natalie pulled her sleeping bag over her face, debating whether or not to break it to Lara that people do breathe while sleeping. Instead, she tried to remain as unconscious-looking as possible, despite her heart beating like a drum.

Could her cousins hear the blood whooshing through her veins or sense the frantic energy crackling through her like a downed powerline?

"You don't want to keep the kiss keeper waiting, Nat!" Leslie whisper-shouted.

"Yeah, it's your turn. Get down off your bunk and meet the keeper," Lara added.

Natalie cracked an eye open and peered down at the girls. Leslie and Lara had managed to rouse their entire cabin without the knowledge of their camp counselor, still sleeping peacefully on the other side of the rectangular room. The campers stood around her bunk in their nightgowns, staring up at her with bedhead and bleary eyes.

It was their last night at Camp Woolwich. Cozied up to the Maine coastline, their grandparents had been running this summer camp since the early seventies when her grandpa, Hal Woolwich, had won the land in a card game.

Her mother and her uncles had grown up here, spending their summers exploring the woods, swimming in the ocean, and sailing the short distance to Woolwich Island, their tiny private island across the cove. And while she hadn't grown up in Maine, she'd spent her childhood summers here as a camper, and now, at thirteen years old, Natalie had moved up from the children's cottage and into the teen girls' cabin.

And boy, oh, boy! Along with the lip gloss and nail polish, the mean girl claws came out!

Back in the children's cottages, nobody would ever think of leaving after lights out. Nope, all those nine to twelve-year-olds were snug, dreaming away in their cots while she looked down on the gathering of hormone-ridden, boy-crazy teen girls congregating near the ladder that led up to her top bunk.

Leslie held a flashlight to her wrist, illuminating her watch. "Come on! It's almost midnight. You don't want to be late."

"Yeah, you don't want to miss your date with your keeper," Lara added.

The kiss keeper. Ugh!

Natalie had about had it with this silly camp legend.

"Natalie Callahan, if you don't drag your ass off that bunk, I'm climbing up there," Leslie hissed.

Natalie ran her hands down her sleep-deprived face. "Fine, I'm coming," she muttered.

Out of all her cousins, Leslie and Lara were the ones closest in age to her.

And in addition to being her kin, they were also the worst human beings ever to walk the surface of the earth.

Okay, maybe not *the* worst, but pretty close.

Leslie clocked in at two years her senior while Lara was barely a year older. But from the way they harped on her, you'd think they were decades older.

Another point of contention—these two had a combined intellect rivaling that of a salad spinner and only cared about two things these days: boys and boys.

Natalie climbed down from her bunk and glanced over at the counselor's bed. But it was no use hoping the woman would wake up. After all the shenanigans her cabinmates had been up to that summer, it was clear that the chick could sleep through World War III.

Nat brushed her hair out of her face as Leslie shoved a pair of rain boots into her chest.

"Put these on. It's time to go," her cousin ordered.

"Why boots?" she questioned.

"Duh." Les scoffed. "You're going out into the woods. You need decent foot protection."

Natalie hugged the boots to her chest and shivered as the chilly night breeze blew in through the window screens. "Do I have to do this? It's kind of stupid."

Leslie gasped. "You know the legend. It's your first summer in the teen girls' cabin, and every newbie has to pay tribute to the Kiss Keeper. It's a camp tradition, and you're the last one, Nat. No more stalling."

"But I won't even know who I'm kissing," she protested, trying to buy herself some time.

Lara grabbed a swath of cloth and tucked it inside one of the boots. "That's the whole point. You go to the old well with your eyes covered and wait for your kiss keeper."

Nat tightened her grip on the boots. "But the kiss keeper is just some guy from the teen boys' cabin."

Leslie stared at the ceiling. "Right, moron! You're his kiss keeper, and he's yours. You've been coming to camp almost as long as we have. You know what you have to do."

Nat stared at the shadows playing on the worn wood plank floor. "But I don't want to kiss anyone."

That wasn't exactly true, but she certainly wasn't about to clue her cousins in on that little tidbit.

"That's why the kiss keeper is so great. It's like it never happened because you don't know who he is, and he doesn't know who you are," Lara offered.

"What if I blurt out my name?" Nat countered.

Leslie pointed the flashlight's beam at her chin. Her nostrils flared as the orange glow illuminated her cousin's face in a demonic shade of orange.

"The last girl who did that is at the bottom of the well," Leslie answered, eyes wide, with all the theatrics afforded to a teenage drama queen.

Natalie let out a long sigh. "I'm pretty sure Grandma and Grandpa would know if there was a camper chilling out at the bottom of the well. I mean, wouldn't she yell up for someone to get her out?"

Leslie groaned and swished her ponytail over her shoulder. "Like always, you're missing the point, Nat."

Lara glanced at her sister, tried to swish her ponytail, then pulled the poorly swished hair out of her mouth. "Yeah, Nat, all you do is climb trees and walk around with that sketchbook, drawing pictures and staring at flowers.

What guy is going to want to hook up with a girl who's totally obsessed with colored pencils?"

Natalie shrugged. "Somebody into art or nature or even pencils?"

Unlike her guy-obsessed cousins, parading around camp in barely-there jean shorts and tank tops, she had no interest in attracting the attention Leslie and Lara craved.

Well...maybe not *no interest.*

After her parents divorced six months ago, her life had split into two parts. Half of it was spent in a tiny town in southern Vermont with her mother not far from her grandma and grandpa Woolwich, while the other half was spent with her father across the country in California. She knew her parents loved her, and the whole situation was quite amicable as far as divorces go.

But she craved to be part of a cohesive unit again—to feel whole again—and not live as this fragmented girl who spent her weekends flying as an unaccompanied minor across the country when an idea sparked on her last flight from California.

Seated next to a newly married couple, all googly-eyed and completely in love, on her flight to camp, she started wondering if a boy could fill that void for her. Then she remembered that a boyfriend would probably want to kiss her. It wasn't like it was a huge deal. Kids at her school would go and kiss behind the bleachers all the time, but she certainly didn't want to kiss a stranger tonight.

Leslie crossed her arms. "You don't have a choice, Nat. It's your turn, and you're going."

"At least, let me change out of my nightgown, Les," she said, conceding to the inevitable.

Another swish of ponytail. "Nope, it's pajamas and the bandana for you, missy," her cousin replied, plucking the square of material from the boot and fashioning it into a blindfold.

"What about when I have to walk back?" she murmured.

"Just don't fall in the well or walk off a cliff. It's not that far. You'll be fine," Lara said with a giggle.

Fine?

Alone and wandering near an abandoned well in the middle of a heavily wooded area off the coast of southern Maine didn't seem like the kind of place a pajama-wearing girl would be fine.

To be totally honest, this whole kiss keeper business constituted the complete opposite of fine.

"Put on your boots," her elder cousin ordered as Nat contemplated a last resort tactic.

She gave her cousin a sugar-sweet smile then dropped the bulky footwear to the floor. The rubber boots hit the ground with a sharp thud as everyone's head swiveled toward the counselor's bunk.

Wake up! Wake up! Wake up!

Natalie channeled all the psychic energy she could into rousing the counselor, and...oh my, God...had it worked?

Her heart nearly stopped as the woman snorted in her sleep while the campers looked on, wide-eyed, and barely breathing.

"Oh, no! Is she...?" Lara began before Leslie clamped her hand over her sister's mouth.

But her little boot stunt was all for nothing. Unaffected by the crash, the counselor rolled onto her side then continued snoring softly.

"Scientists should study this woman's uncanny sleep skills," Nat said, her shoulders slumping forward as the hint of a smug grin pulled at the corners of Leslie's mouth.

Her cousin shined the beam of light into her eyes like a

seasoned interrogator. "Put on the boots, then turn around. Pull another stunt like that, and we'll send you out in your underwear."

Natalie tried to bat the light away and catch the eye of any of the other girls, hoping to find an ally. But nobody dared to defy Leslie Woolwich. The girl seemed to know how to kiss up to her grandparents to always get out of trouble.

Nat released a low, resigned sigh then pulled on her boots, and before she was even upright again, Leslie didn't miss a beat and secured the bandana around her head with an extra little tug.

"Good luck, Nat," Lara whispered through giggles as Leslie led her out of the cabin and onto the trail leading to the well.

Their feet crunched along the path littered with pine needles, and Natalie tried to slow her breathing. She knew that the kiss keeper was a childish legend, but the boy making his way to the well was going to be very much real—and she'd never even practiced kissing before. Sure, she'd kissed her mother and father, but that was on the cheek.

Her mouth went dry, and she licked her lips.

What if she ran out of saliva and she and whoever her kiss keeper was got stuck together?

What if he bit her or tried to feel her up?

A million nightmare scenarios tumbled through her mind when she nearly fell to the ground. Luckily, Leslie grabbed the collar of her nightgown and kept her upright.

"You'll walk from here on your own, Nat. Keep going straight and stay on the path."

"How will I know I'm there?" she asked, suddenly, for the first time all summer, craving her cousin's company.

Leslie hadn't always been so awful. When they were

younger, they were inseparable when they were in the children's cottage together. But that seemed like lightyears ago.

"You'll either fall into the well or bump into it. I'd suggest bumping into it," Les answered through a yawn.

"And the guy?" Nat asked, working to keep her voice steady.

"Yeah? What about him?"

"I have to kiss him?" she asked, knowing it was a stupid question.

Leslie let out a weary huff. "Yes, this is not something to mess around with, Nat. This is like ghosts and legends and shit."

The girl wasn't wrong. The way they told the story around the campfire was that, years ago, there was a lighthouse not far from Camp Woolwich. That part was legit. And while the campers weren't supposed to leave the camp property, to this day, kids would still sneak away to explore the crumbling relic. It's the next part that Nat had trouble wrapping her mind around.

"You know it will upset Otis if every girl in the teen cabin doesn't offer up a kiss to the keeper," Leslie continued.

Otis.

"Who was he again?" Natalie asked, hoping her cousin would take the bait and keep talking.

"Seriously, Nat? You need to stop climbing trees, pull your head out of your sketchbook, and pay attention."

Natalie crossed her fingers behind her back, hoping her know-it-all cousin would keep talking.

"Fine, here's the story—because you need to understand why this is so important," Leslie began.

"Thanks, Les," she murmured, grateful for another few minutes.

"All right, Otis Wiscasset was the only son of the man

who used to run the old lighthouse a gazillion years ago. He was supposed to take over for his father, but Otis had other ideas. Kissing ideas," her cousin added.

"I think I remember that part. Keep going," Nat replied, wondering how long she could stall. Maybe after Les recounted the Kiss Keeper Tale, she could ask her about nail polish or push-up bras.

"One summer night," Leslie continued. "It's said that Otis Wiscasset and Muriel Boothe were supposed to meet at the well to have their first kiss and then run off together. But the Boothe family was all hoity-toity rich and didn't want their daughter attached to a lowly lighthouse keeper's son. Well, on the night Otis and Muriel had planned to meet at the well to have their first kiss and then elope, Muriel didn't show up. It's said that her parents had put her on a boat back to stay with relatives in England to keep them apart. Otis was delirious with the grief of not ever kissing Muriel. He cursed this well, then disappeared. And now, every summer, all the Camp Woolwich teen girls have to meet their kiss keeper at the well and offer a kiss to appease the Kiss Keeper—or else."

"Or else, what?" Nat asked.

"Jesus, Nat!" her cousin exclaimed, then bonked the side of her head. "You know this! If you take off the blindfold or don't offer up a kiss, you'll have bad luck, and you'll never find true love, blah, blah, blah! You have to do it."

"Are you going to follow me?" Natalie asked, hating the treacherous shake in her voice.

Leslie bumped her shoulder. "Hell no! Do you think I want to watch you and some loser lock lips?"

But before she could get in another word or ask another question to stall the inevitable, the sound of Leslie's flip-flops clip-clopping down the path faded away as her cousin booked-it back to the teen girls' cabin. Natalie took a steadying breath, her senses heightening, as the forest came alive. The scent of the salty sea and wild blackberries washed over her while insect chirps and frog calls peppered the air as she carefully took one tentative step, then another, then another.

"Calm down," she whispered, her voice cutting through the nocturnal soundscape.

She knew these trails. She'd sketched a blackberry bush near here just the other day. And, as far as the well, it was simply a circular rock formation with a little wooden roof. Nothing scary. Nothing out of the ordinary. But when the wind picked up and whistled through the thick Maine foliage, her rational brain took a back seat to that little part of her that believed in the folklore of the Kiss Keeper.

Was the ghost of Otis Wiscasset out here, waiting to collect his summer kisses? Was there someone behind her? A spirit? A ghoul? Were they all skin and bones, floating inches above the ground, glowing in that horror movie haunting shade of electric blue? Her pulse kicked up when a voice brought her spiraling thoughts to a screeching halt.

"Um...hello?"

Nat startled as a shiver spider-crawled the length of her spine, and panic flooded her system.

She stretched out her arms, waving them this way and that. "Is that you, Otis?"

It was real! It was real! It was real!

Holy cow! Her cousins were right!

She turned left, then right, then caught her booted toe on a hard tree root and pitched forward, falling into the arms of—not a ghost.

"No, I'm...the guy," the voice in the darkness said as two hands gripped her shoulders.

Even though she was wearing a blindfold, Nat squeezed her eyes shut, not wanting to invoke the Kiss Keeper Curse.

"I'm...the girl," she answered with her hands pressed to his chest.

Whoever her kiss keeper was, he was tall, and while he wasn't super muscular, he wasn't scrawny either.

Who could it be? Unfortunately, it wasn't like she could even guess. Yes, she'd thought about what it would be like to have a boyfriend. But once she'd arrived at camp—the one place in the world that made her feel whole—she'd focused on her art and sketching and had barely glanced at any of the boys. She wasn't even sure she could name all the girls in her own cabin.

"Are you still wearing your blindfold?" he asked, his thumb brushing past her collarbone and setting off the butterflies in her belly.

She sucked in a sharp breath. "Yeah. Aren't you?"

"I am. I am," he shot back quickly with an apprehensive tinge to his words.

Good. At least, he was nervous, too.

"This is weird, right?" she offered.

His thumb stilled, and his grip on her shoulders relaxed a fraction. "It's really weird."

If this were her normal life, she'd jump back, out of this stranger's near embrace. But this wasn't a stranger. It was her kiss keeper, and oddly, she didn't want him to let go.

"Have you ever kissed anyone?" she asked.

He swallowed hard. "Have you?"

She smiled into the darkness. "I asked first."

Her kiss keeper chuckled, and the nervous edge in his voice disappeared.

"No, I've never kissed anyone before."

Relief calmed her frayed nerves. If she were a terrible kisser, at least, he wouldn't know.

"Should we do it?" she asked, now the one swallowing back her trepidation.

"I think we have to. You know, the legend and all that."

She nodded. "We don't want to upset Otis."

"And my balls," he blurted.

"Your what?" she threw back, not sure she heard him correctly.

Her kiss keeper shifted his weight. "The guys said that if I didn't kiss you, my balls would shrivel up into raisins, and for the rest of my life, my voice would sound like I'd sucked in a lungful of helium."

She pressed her lips together, trying to hold back a laugh, but even her dry mouth couldn't restrain her reaction.

"That's not part of the legend," she said with a giggle, then rested her forehead against his chest. He felt nice. Solid. It was as if the world could shift off its axis, and they'd remain untouched, cocooned in darkness and the Kiss Keeper's protection.

"It's not?" he asked, and she could feel his heartbeat slow.

"No."

"Thank God," he answered in a relieved breath, then stilled. "But the whole never finding your soul mate stuff, is that true?"

She nodded. "Yeah, that's the way I've always heard it."

"And I can't look at you? That's part of it, too," he questioned.

"If you see me, the story goes that I'll be trapped at the bottom of the well—which may be a better alternative to high school—but it would probably suck when it rained."

"Or snowed," he added.

"It's probably best if I remained on the surface of the planet."

Her kiss keeper chuckled again, and his kind voice smoothed out the last of her frayed nerves.

"You're funny," he said as his thumb moved back and forth across her collarbone. An unconscious movement, but she liked it, nonetheless.

Nat steadied herself. "You're nicer than I'd expected."

While her gaze was met with a blanket of darkness, thanks to the blindfold, she could sense that he was smiling.

"You are saving me from a life of tiny testicles and talking like a choir soprano. So, I kind of owe you," he answered with a gentle lilt to his words, confirming his grin as the air grew heavy with anticipation.

A fizzy buzz, ripe with sweet anticipation, replaced the trepidation in her chest. "We couldn't have that," she answered, her breaths growing shallow.

This was it. She was about to have her first kiss.

With her hands pressed to his chest, she felt his heartbeat, strong and steady, as the sound of their breathing slowed, and their breaths mingled in the night air.

"Should we do it?" he whispered.

She swallowed. "You mean kiss?"

She could feel him nod.

"Is it okay if I kissed you?"

"I don't think we have a choice," she replied.

He brushed his thumb across her collarbone. "Can I tell you something?"

"Sure. Anything," she answered, the anticipation near palpable.

"I'd want to kiss you even if we didn't have to," he said with the smile back in his voice.

She matched his grin with one of her own. "You would?"

"Do I sound like an idiot?"

She gently twisted the fabric of his T-shirt. "No, you don't sound like an idiot because I think I'd like to kiss you, too—and not because we want to save your balls or avoid a kiss curse."

He slid his hands from her shoulders up to her face and cupped her cheeks. "This kissing business may be tricky since we can't see each other."

She pushed up onto her tiptoes. "Is this better?"

His chest heaved with a tight exhale.

"Yeah," he answered, leaning in and lowering his head.

His nose brushed against hers as their shallow breaths met in the tiny slice of space that separated their lips. She pushed up farther onto her tippy toes, ready to kiss the kindest boy she'd ever met when the sharp crack of a snapped branch tore through their pre-kiss bubble.

"Is somebody there? You know nobody's supposed to be out here past lights out!" came a deep, irritated voice.

"Shit," her kiss keeper whispered, then grabbed her hand, pulling her away from the well and off the trail.

Shit was right! Camp night patrol—counselors who roamed the property in search of kids sneaking out—had gotten wind of them.

He gripped her hand. "We need to go. We need to get back to our cabins."

She swallowed back her nerves. "But I can't take off this blindfold. I can't look at you."

He drummed his fingers against the back of her hand. "You won't have to. I've got a plan. You'll keep your blindfold on, but I'll need to take mine off to get you back to your cabin. We need to be smart. If they find us together, we're totally screwed."

He was totally right. What would her grandparents think?

"Okay, I'm good with that," she answered.

They had no other option.

He gave her hand a little squeeze. "I'm taking my blindfold off."

A shiver passed through her—or maybe it was the spirit of Otis Wiscasset.

"Okay, let's go," he said, lacing his fingers with hers and leading her into the forest before she could worry any more about ghosts and legends.

They wove their way through the thick foliage, past blackberry bushes and spiny jack pines that covered the property. Sightless, she relied on her kiss keeper until another snapped twig caught her attention.

She tugged his hand. "Stop," she whispered as the sounds of the counselors' voices drew closer.

"Get down," he shot back, guiding her to the ground.

She crouched next to him, and their shoulders pressed together.

"They're close. I can hear them," she whispered.

"We'll let them pass, and then we'll go," he whispered back as the footsteps drew closer and closer.

"Do you see anyone?" another male voice asked.

"Nah. It could have been a fox or a raccoon. I thought I caught something moving out of the corner of my eye."

The men stopped on the other side of the blackberry bush, and Natalie held her breath.

"Let's walk the main loop first, then head past the teen cabins. I'm as tired as fuck and want to get this patrol over."

Nat relaxed as the men continued on. The teen cabins were on the periphery of the property, while the main loop would take the men back toward the heart of the camp.

They had time to get to their cabins—not much—but enough if they hurried.

Her kiss keeper came to the same realization. After the sound of the patrollers' steps disappeared, he was back, whispering in her ear.

"I can get you to your cabin. We've got a couple of minutes. Are you ready?" he asked, helping her to her feet.

"Okay, just let me know if there are any rocks or tree roots to step over. I don't want to fall."

He squeezed her hand. "I won't let you fall."

She wished she could see his face—see if what she saw in his eyes matched what she felt in her heart.

He gave her hand another squeeze, then led her through the forest. He was smart to stay off the path, and within what felt like both seconds and days, he came to a stop.

"We're here. Put out your hand."

She reached forward with the hand not holding his and felt the scratch of the screened-in windows.

"Thank—" she began, but before she could finish, lips pressed down on hers, silencing her, capturing her.

Her kiss keeper's lips.

Her first kiss.

She grabbed a handful of his T-shirt, and his hand returned to rest on her shoulder. His thumb brushed over her collarbone in sweet, gentle strokes as she parted her lips and dared to allow her tongue to peek out.

"Wow!" he breathed, sounding caught off guard as his tongue met hers.

French kissing.

She was French kissing the sweetest guy on the planet.

Tidal waves and fireworks collided with a great surge of energy, sending her pulse into overdrive and igniting a strange, delicious stirring deep within her belly. She wanted to be closer to this boy. She wanted to kiss him until the sun came up—maybe longer. Everything seemed possible with his lips pressed to hers until the unmistakable snort of her counselor rang out. Her kiss keeper pulled back, but he stood there as still as the night.

Was he looking at her? Was he grossed out? Did she do it wrong? It didn't feel wrong!

"That kiss was better than sailing across the lake," he said as wonder wove its way through his words.

But before she could reply, he released her hand and ran off into the night.

Amped up on hormones, fear, and excitement, she forced herself to count to thirty before pulling off the blindfold and staring out into the inky darkness.

Her kiss keeper had disappeared.

She pressed her fingers to her still-tingling lips and leaned against the side of the cabin.

It happened. It really happened. She'd kissed her...

Nat gasped, and panic shot through her body.

They'd kissed—but not at the well.

Were they cursed?

Did that kiss even count? Had they blown their chance at finding true love? Was her kiss keeper destined to a life singing soprano?

She sighed, then stared up at the starry night sky.

Only time would tell.

1

"Maybe you're cursed, Nat."

Natalie shot up from where she was organizing a stack of sketchbooks on the floor and knocked over a coffee can, jam-packed with her students' paintbrushes.

"Why would you say that?" she asked, looking up at her friend, Tera, one of the first-grade teachers at the school where she'd gotten hired on as the temporary art teacher last fall.

Tera ran her fingertips along the rows of pastels—all counted and ready to be stored away until the children returned to school in the fall.

"I thought it was a pain to pack up my classroom at the end of the school year. But Sweet Jesus! Look at all this! This is like the definition of insanity!" she remarked, attempting to pick up a plastic tub teeming with markers.

Nat gathered the loose brushes from the floor. "You do remember that I have to teach every child in the school. From kindergarten to fifth grade, they all get to see my smiling face?"

Tera flipped through a towering mass of drawings. "And

God love ya for it, Miss Callahan! I can barely handle my twenty-four."

"Lucky for you, I love my job," Nat answered with a chuckle, staring out at the little tables and stools dotting the sun-dappled space.

Tera sauntered over to the other side of the classroom and held up a lump of clay that was either a mug or a sculpture of a bowel movement. With third-grade boys, it honestly could have been either.

"This is art?" she asked with a playful expression.

"Mistakes and imperfections are part of the process," Natalie answered, tapping the little sign on her desk with her grandma Woolwich's motto painted in curly lettering.

"Well, we're not making the mistake of missing out on the staff party. Come on, art teacher! The custodian is making her world-famous lime sherbet and Sprite punch. It's about to get crazy up in this elementary school."

Nat held up a finger. "Hold on! Let me put these paintbrushes away first."

She grabbed the can and surveyed the empty classroom. All the supplies were neatly lined up along the counter that ran the length of the art room. She placed the paintbrushes —the last item to be packed up—into a plastic tub with the rest of the painting materials and lovingly touched the tips of the brushes as thoughts of her grandma Woolwich came to mind.

An accomplished painter and sculptor, her grandmother had fostered her love of art from an early age. She'd spent summer after summer at her grandmother's side, watching the woman transform a snow-white canvas into a rocky Maine coastline with a few strokes of a brush or take a lump of clay and work it into an intricate vase.

Over those lazy summer days, she'd learned that, in the

pursuit of art, beauty could be found everywhere. And no matter how many times she'd observed her grandma Bev at work, witnessing the transformation of a blank slate becoming a vivid masterpiece left her spellbound. And when it was her time to choose an area of study in college, the artists' path was her only choice.

Natalie placed the lid on the supply bin and sighed. Maybe her luck had changed. After a string of working a slew of temporary positions in Kansas, Utah, Texas, and now Colorado as a long-term elementary art substitute teacher, filling in for instructors on leaves of absence, maybe this school would be the one where she'd get to stay and put down roots. She'd heard whispers that the former art teacher wasn't going to return after her maternity leave. Unfortunately, nothing had been announced officially.

But it wasn't just the hope of steady employment in the field she loved that had her smiling a little more brightly than usual.

Her lackluster love life was looking up, too.

"Speaking of *other* mistakes and imperfections, how's your Jake? You're on Jake number two, right?" Tera asked, cutting into her little daydream.

Nat's cheeks heated. It was the second guy named Jake she'd dated since she'd started working at the school and the sixth Jake she'd gone out with since she'd graduated from college six years ago. But she wasn't about to cop to that. Jake or Jacob was a common enough name. It couldn't be that weird that she'd dated a half dozen of them.

"Jake's great!" she answered, smiling as she secured the plastic lid.

He did seem pretty great. Jake number six, not that she ever called him or any other Jake by a number, traveled a lot for his work as a pharmaceutical sales rep. But he'd agreed to clear his schedule for an entire week to come with her to Maine for her grandparents' fiftieth wedding anniversary, being held at Camp Woolwich.

And oh, how she was ready to return to the trails and fresh sea air where she'd spent her summers growing up.

Thanks to her chaotic schedule and a paycheck that barely covered the rent, it had been nearly ten years since she'd last returned to enjoy Maine in the summertime. To earn a little extra cash over the years, she'd taken on some freelance graphic design projects which took up much of her time during the summer and over holidays.

Still, fifty years of marriage was something to be celebrated, and she was thrilled when an airline voucher arrived with her grandparents' invitation, along with a handwritten note from her grandmother encouraging her to bring a date to the celebration. Everything seemed to be falling into place. At twenty-eight years old, she craved finding a love like the bond shared between her grandparents. The kind of love that maybe, just maybe, she could find with Jake number six—not that she ever called him that.

Tera lifted her large portfolio bag propped against her suitcase.

"You're bringing art supplies on vacation? The last thing I want to see over my summer break is school supplies," her friend said, eyeing her closely.

"Teaching art and creating art are two very different things. I haven't painted or sketched for myself in ages. I was hoping to get back to it when I'm in Maine. I've missed it so much."

Tera unzipped the canvas bag and gasped. "Oh, my! What art project requires these?"

Her friend swung a lacy black G-string around her finger.

"Put that back, Tera!" Nat shrieked. "That's for Jake!"

"Jake wears lingerie? Wowza! I'd never pegged you as one for the kinky stuff," Tera answered, pulling out the matching lacy bra.

Nat bolted across the room and snagged the sexy undergarments. "I was going to do the whole high heels and a trench coat with only lingerie beneath for the plane ride."

Tera's jaw dropped. "You? Little Miss Art Smock is going to try to pull a sexy trench-capade?"

She glanced down at her dress that, unfortunately, could best be described as an art smock.

This wardrobe switcheroo may be the craziest thing she'd ever done, but something in the back of her mind kept telling her she needed to up her game with Jake number six —not that she called him that.

Natalie slid the slinky underwear into the bag next to her fire engine red open-toe high heels. "I was going to change once I got to the airport and throw my dress and sandals into my suitcase before I checked it. Do you think I'm crazy?"

"No way! It might be fun to spice it up and cut the tension. You are bringing a boy home to meet the family. This is big, Natalie."

It was a big deal. She and Jake had been dating for five months and six days. They hadn't done the whole *I love you* bit yet, but maybe this trip would take their relationship to the next level.

"Which reminds me. I need to text him," she said.

Nat pulled her cell from her pocket to find no new texts and tried to ignore the twist in her belly. The plan was for Jake to fly back into Denver, meet her at the airport, and then the two of them would fly off to Maine together. He'd been out of town all week and hadn't replied when she'd texted him this morning, trying to confirm where they'd meet at the airport. That sinking feeling doubled when she scrolled through her text feed to find that he hadn't responded to any of her messages that week. It had been so crazy, finishing up the final few days of the school year, that she hadn't noticed until now.

She glanced at her friend, then hammered out a quick text.

Can't wait to see you! Text me when you get this!

That was fine, right? Not too clingy or desperate? They were about to travel more than halfway across the country together and spend a week with her family. Meals had been planned, and a headcount had been taken to ensure enough seating, food, and drinks for the event. It wasn't strange or obsessive to try to confirm that.

She ignored the sinking feeling and hit send.

"You're making a face," Tera said, crossing her arms.

"It's nothing," she answered, pocketing her phone.

"It's something. I usually make that face when I have to interact with my stepmother or any other member of my extended family."

Extended family.

Oh, no!

Leslie and Lara's stupid smug faces flashed in Nat's mind.

Tera cringed. "Oh my, God! You must be thinking about your family."

Nat waved her off. "Most of them are great."

"But?" Tera threw out.

Natalie sighed. "But I have two cousins who I've never really gotten along with that are going to be there, too."

Tera's eyes went wide. "Wait! Are these the podiatrist sisters who each married a podiatrist? The ones where both the guys asked to see your feet before they married your cousins?"

Natalie cocked her head to the side. "How do you know about that?"

"Happy hour, like three months ago. You know, the one with the bottomless margaritas," Tera replied.

Nat's stomach was back in knots. "Oh, that's right! And that's why I barely drink. I'm a complete lightweight," she replied, remembering the tequila haze, and the next morning spent nursing an epic hangover.

Tera grinned. "And you're a huge drunk-talker! So, it's true? You have to spend a week with your two evil podiatrist step-cousins and their creepy foot fetish husbands?"

Natalie sighed. "Sadly, they're blood-related cousins, not step-cousins. And yes, they'll all be there. At least, I don't have to room with them like when we were kids at summer camp. My grandparents are putting us up in the individual rental cabins on the property."

Tera glanced down at her feet. "I hope you've got several pairs of closed-toe shoes in that suitcase."

Nat wiggled her exposed toes. "I'm way ahead of you. Besides those heels, these are the only sandals I'm bringing. I've got three pairs of closed-toe shoes in my suitcase. And I only plan on wearing sandals with a super-long maxi dress to keep my little piggies hidden away."

The women broke into laughter as Nat did another piggy wiggle demonstration when a knock at the door startled them.

"Hey! The lime sherbet punch is almost gone! I wanted to make sure you got some, Miss Callahan," came a friendly male voice.

Jack Leeman, the school's golden-haired gym teacher, stood in her doorway, grinning at her like a puppy dog.

"*Miss Callahan* and I will be down in a second, Jack," Tera answered, biting back a very un-puppy-doggish grin.

The man nodded and headed down the hall, like a golden retriever who'd gotten a *that's a good boy* pat on the head.

Tera came to her side. "You could always have Jack if things with Jake didn't work out."

"You're terrible," Natalie replied, setting her purse and art tote on the roller bag. She'd need to leave for the airport right after the faculty celebration.

"Well, he might be your type, too," Tera said, her tone growing mischievous, as they headed toward the lounge. "When you look at all the letters in their names, Jack is pretty close to Jake. But Jack has a short vowel *A* sound while Jake has a nice *long* vowel. Do you like your vowels like you like your Jakes, Miss Callahan? Hard and long?"

"Hard and long! Those are two excellent words to describe our Miss Callahan."

The women gasped as the school's principal, Mr. Lutz, poked his head out of the staff workroom.

Natalie stiffened—and not in the long and hard way, but the nervous and humiliated one.

She pasted on a smile. "Sorry, sir, we were just..."

"We were discussing long and short vowel lessons and how to incorporate art into teaching the concept," Tera offered, swooping in.

"You both are always putting your students first," the man replied, ushering them into the packed room.

"Thank you, Mr. Lutz," Natalie said as Tera made a beeline for the punch bowl.

Nat started to head over when the principal tapped her arm. "Since you've joined our staff, Miss Callahan, you've always worked hard and put in long hours. And I'm not sure if you know this, but Mrs. Ford, our regular art teacher, isn't coming back."

Natalie's heart jumped into her throat. Was he about to ask her to stay on as the school's permanent art teacher?

"Mr. Lutz, it's time for your speech," the school secretary called and gestured to her watch.

The principal pulled a note card from his pocket. "One moment, Miss Callahan. I do have something else I need to discuss with you privately. Can you stick around after my little speech?"

"Of course," she replied, holding herself back from doing cartwheels, then wove her way through the staff to stand next to Tera.

"Did he ask you to stay on? I just heard that Ford's not coming back?" her friend said, handing her a paper cup of the green punch.

Nat gathered herself. "Not yet, but he did say that I've done a great job and that he wants to talk with me."

Tera raised her cup. "You've got to be a shoo-in!"

How she wanted to believe that! How she wanted to fist-bump her way through the room, high-fiving each teacher in the faculty lounge like they were in the winning team's locker room after the World Series. But one too many times in her life, she'd gotten her hopes up only to have them crash down upon her.

Was she cursed?

With each failed "Jake" relationship and each promising job that didn't last, it was hard not to think that Otis Wiscasset hadn't unleashed the Kiss Keeper Curse on her when she was thirteen.

The bright side. At least, she wasn't living at the bottom of a well.

Tera gestured with her chin toward the front of the

room. "Hey, Principal Lutz said he's got a big announcement."

Nat pushed her Kiss Keeper Curse worries away and focused on the rest of the man's speech.

"Finally, we're here today to celebrate an end to a wonderful school year and the many teachers who worked so hard to ensure that our students continue to love learning, and I've got some terrific news, folks," Principal Lutz began.

Natalie downed the rest of her punch. She couldn't have a dry, cracked voice when she thanked the principal for offering her a full-time, vested position as the school's official art teacher.

Mr. Lutz smiled broadly. "That grant came in for us, and we have the funds to put in a brand-new play structure."

The staff erupted into cheers as side conversations broke out, and Principal Lutz melted into the crowd of educators.

Natalie forced herself to take a breath.

Okay, that wasn't a bad thing. The school could use a new playground.

But what about the art teacher position?

She glanced at Tera.

Her friend patted her arm. "Heads up. Lutz is coming your way."

"Miss Callahan, may I have a word with you in the hall?"

Oh, no!

In school-speak, *a word in the hallway* was never good. But it couldn't always be bad. Perhaps, he wanted privacy when offering her the art teacher position. He was just being a gentleman in case she was so overcome with excitement she fainted.

Nat's pulse kicked into overdrive.

OMG! This wasn't a Victorian novella.

She shared a nervous look with Tera, then followed the man out into the dreaded hallway.

"Miss Callahan, you've been such an asset to our staff."

This was a good start.

Natalie gave him her best Mary Poppins, lover of children and spoons full of sugar smile. "It's been such an honor teaching here. You've got an amazing staff, and the children and their families have been wonderful to work with."

Mr. Lutz's expression softened. "That's what makes telling you this so hard, Miss Callahan."

The district pulled our arts funding.

I wish we could keep you, but we don't have the money in the budget.

Despite nodding and putting on a brave face, Natalie didn't hear much more as the image of the Kiss Keeper's well flashed through her mind, and the dream of finding a permanent teaching position spiraled down the drain.

2

Jake Teller glanced out at the packed auditorium, took note of the blonde with the killer cleavage in the front row, then strode across the stage. His long legs consumed the space as the spotlight lit his enviable physique in golden light.

"Guilt and remorse have no place in the world of business. Bullshit thoughts of karma and yin and yang only serve to hold you back. Take my advice. Work every angle you've got and stick to the black and white. The numbers, the statistics, the reports. Anybody who tells you that they go by their gut alone when it comes to buying multi-million-dollar commercial real estate is a damn fool and should not be someone you choose to keep in your confidence."

He watched as the participants eagerly took notes, many holding up cell phones and recording his talk. He'd be the first to admit that industry symposiums and speaking events were one percent substance and ninety-nine percent fluff. But it looked good to have his name, and the name of the company he worked for, Linton Holdings, splashed all over the industry he was itching to conquer.

There was an ethical line, sure, but nothing in the realm

of real estate negotiations was carved into stone. He lived his life a breath away from that tipping point, teetering on the edge. Careful to keep his hands just clean enough.

He stopped and stared out at the crowd. "And never fall in love with a property. Attachment is an emotion best left to the weak," he added as the click of hundreds of people typing his words verbatim onto their laptops crackled and popped through the cavernous space.

At twenty-eight years old, he was the youngest development VP at Linton. And more important than that, a favorite of the founder himself, billionaire hotel and real estate developer, Charlie Linton.

Eager to prove himself to the self-made tycoon who'd been in the game for fifty years, he'd traveled the globe, procuring the perfect properties for an even better price. Dubai, Hong Kong, Montenegro, it didn't matter the country or continent. With a head for numbers and the ability to see trends before they peaked, he'd demonstrated not only his intelligence but his hunger.

Jake Teller was in it for the kill, and that's why he was the best.

He eyed the cleavage in the front row, and the woman took notice. She ran her tongue across her top lip, then uncrossed and crossed her legs, allowing her already short skirt to ride up her thighs with the sensual movement.

He bit back a grin. Symposiums were great for picking up a quick screw in some generic hotel room, and he followed the same principles with relationships as he did in business.

Well, using the term *relationship* was a bit of a stretch.

Could he give a woman a night of immeasurable pleasure?

Absolutely.

Would he be there in the morning to cook her breakfast? Hell no.

Rule number one, just like in real estate, never fall in love.

The guy in the sound booth signaled for him to wrap it up, and Jake gazed out into the packed room, ready to go out on a bang, and then meet up with the chick in the front row to do the same—multiple times.

"Properties will come and go. Be tenacious. Be relentless and keep your heart out of it." He met the blonde's gaze. "Don't give an inch until you're completely satisfied. That's the way you get ahead in the big leagues of commercial real estate."

The crowd clapped, and he absorbed the adulation. He wasn't a trust fund baby born with a silver spoon in his mouth. Everything he'd gotten in this life had been by his own volition.

The lights came on, and a stagehand rushed over and removed the mic from his lapel. As the auditorium cleared out, he caught sight of the blonde, lingering at the end of the row. Now, this was the way to end a day of presentations. He walked off the stage and headed her way. She straightened up and gave him one hell of a *you're about to get laid* grin when someone else caught his eye. Someone vastly more important than a piece of convention ass.

His mentor. His teacher. The man he'd emulated since the day he got hired on at Linton Holdings.

Charlie Linton.

He passed the blonde without a second glance and extended his hand. "If I'd known you were coming, I would have gotten you a seat up front."

"Next to that?" the man asked, gesturing with his chin

toward the blonde who hadn't yet realized that she'd become inconsequential.

"Nothing wrong with a little company," Jake tossed back.

Charlie chuckled. "But you see, Jake. If I'd let you know I was coming, you would have offered for me to do the presentation with you, and I wanted to watch you, unguarded."

"Fair enough. How'd I do, boss?" he asked, but he already knew the answer.

Charlie narrowed his gaze. "Like always, you nailed it. There's not a councilman, sultan, or senator you can't get on your side. I knew you had the balls for this racket after you closed the deal on that high-rise in Dubai. Do you remember that project?"

Of course, he remembered. But the fact that Charlie remembered it, with his myriad of business deals going on at any one moment, was what spoke volumes.

Pride glimmered in the man's eyes. "I'd sent all my senior people over, thinking it was a slam-dunk deal. But after three months of negotiations, they hadn't gained an inch. That's when you came to me, Jake. Christ! What were you? Twenty-five?"

"Twenty-three," he corrected.

"Twenty-fucking-three," Charlie repeated, shaking his head. "You asked if you could take a shot at Dubai. I thought it was youthful ignorance. If ten of my top people—half of them my damn nephews—couldn't pull off a half a billion-dollar deal, then how the hell could a kid fresh out of college do it."

Jake kept his features neutral as Charlie watched him closely, the crinkles in the corners of his eyes deepening.

"In less than twenty-four hours after you landed in the

United Arab Emirates, you called to tell me you'd sealed the deal."

Jake shrugged off the accomplishment. "I just happened to know that the Sheikh heading up Dubai's development council liked basketball. After a few games of one-on-one, he was ready to come to the table."

Charlie shook his head as a sly grin pulled at the corners of his mouth. "It wasn't only the basketball. I saw your notes. You'd researched their entire negotiation team. You'd scoured their social media profiles. You knew them inside and out. You knew what they wanted, and you knew how to use that to get me what I wanted."

"Rolling in with the Linton name doesn't hurt either," Jake replied.

Yes, he'd single-handedly closed a huge deal, but nobody liked a loudmouthed braggart.

Charlie continued to study him with a hawkish eye. "You and I both know it wasn't only my name that got us that deal. Despite that cocksure presentation you did, you're persuasive without being a prick. You know how to work a room. You come in knowing what levers to pull. You do your goddamn homework."

"You taught me that, Charlie. I owe my success to you, and I'll always put Linton Holdings first," he said, keeping his voice steady.

The walk down memory lane was over as Charlie's inquisitive demeanor changed to one of the driven and ruthless negotiator. At seventy-five years old, the man still commanded respect and a healthy dose of fear from anyone who dared get in his way.

"I'm glad to hear you say that because I have a special job for you, Jake. There's a piece of land I'd like for you to acquire."

"I'm your man. I can be on a plane to anywhere in less than an hour. Where to next? Just this morning, I got a tip from a local politician that the market is heating up in Spain. Is that where you'd like me to go?" he asked.

Charlie shook his head. "I got a tip, too. But it's not about Spain. It's about Maine."

The breath caught in Jake's throat. At the mention of Maine, his stoic demeanor nearly cracked.

He cleared his throat. "Maine? Like trees and barely a high-rise or luxury resort to be found? That Maine?"

Why the hell would Charlie want to send him there? Linton projects fell in the hundreds of millions—even billion-dollar range. What would be the point of dropping that kind of money in a location that was barely a blip on their development radar?

Charlie gave him a slap on the shoulder. "That's the one, my boy. I want you to procure a piece of land a little north of Portland near the coast called Woolwich Cove. There's currently a camp on the property that goes by the name Camp Woolwich," Charlie said, contempt infused into the words, but Jake couldn't focus on the man's darkening expression and willed himself not to break out into a cold sweat.

Camp Woolwich was the last place he'd been before his world had turned upside down. The last summer where he believed that life was fair and that kids couldn't have all the things they loved taken from them in the blink of an eye.

Charlie's hawkish gaze was back. "You look like you've seen a ghost. Have you heard of Camp Woolwich?"

Oh, there was a ghost. A ghost named Otis Wiscasset.

He'd have to do a better job at muting his emotions. Charlie didn't miss much, and he sure as hell wasn't about to break down and share his sad childhood tale.

A muscle ticked in Jake's jaw as he worked to keep the sentiment from his voice. "I spent a summer there when I was a kid."

Charlie's face lit up with an odd, gleeful expression, bordering on a mad scientist level of excitement. "You've been there? On the property?"

Jake glanced away. "I haven't been there since I was thirteen. But yes, I remember a few things about it."

That was a lie.

He remembered more than a few things.

He remembered a well, surrounded by the forest and cast in darkness, where he'd held the hand of the first girl he'd kissed. He didn't even know her name or what she looked like. That kiss keeper bullshit and his blindfolded trek through the woods had turned out to be the last happy memory of his childhood.

He could still feel the adrenaline coursing through his veins as he and his kiss keeper held hands and dodged the camp night patrol. And then he'd done it. He'd kissed her outside her cabin. They were supposed to lock lips at the well to offer a kiss as some way to thwart his balls falling off or some crazy campfire folktale. But that night, he knew he couldn't leave without kissing the most enchanting girl he'd ever met.

Where was she now?

Even with all the money and the one-night stands he'd accumulated over the years, he couldn't think of anything he'd desired more than when he'd wanted to kiss that young girl with her face obscured by a damn bandana blindfold.

But he knew one thing for sure. He couldn't go back to Maine and risk the wounds of his past ripping open. He'd spent too much time fortifying himself from feeling anything to risk having all his defenses crumble once he set foot in that place.

Charlie clapped his hands with a hard slap, pulling Jake back from the past. "This is excellent, Jake. You already have a grasp of the place."

Jake shook his head, a minute movement to get himself back on track.

"Is it still owned by Mr. and Mrs. Woolwich? I think their names were Hal and Betty."

"Hal and Beverly. She goes by Bev," Charlie corrected with that odd, sharp edge.

"That's right, Hal and Bev," he repeated, treading carefully.

It was surprising to see Charlie so agitated over something as mundane as him forgetting a name. Charlie never cared about the lives of the players in a deal—only that it went his way.

"Have you had anyone reach out to them and see if they were interested in selling?" he asked, steering the conversation in a more business-oriented direction.

From what he remembered, the camp founders loved the place. They'd built their lives there. Raised their family there. There were so many Woolwich grandchildren, nieces, and nephews, he was never able to figure out who was who.

Charlie made a face as if he'd sucked a lemon. "I've had a handful of my nephews look into it quietly, never mentioning the Linton name, but damn old Hal Woolwich will barely speak a word to them, let alone allow them on the property."

"What makes you think they'd even consider selling?" Jake pressed.

"Two things. They're not running the camp program this summer, which leads me to believe that there may be some financial constraints, making them more vulnerable and amenable to selling," Charlie answered, the edge in his voice replaced with his usual cool detachment.

"And the other thing?" Jake asked.

Charlie gave him a hint of a smile. "Just a little information shared with me privately."

Jake crossed his arms. "What makes you think they'll talk to me?"

"For one thing, you're a former camper. I don't know if that'll be enough to get you in the door, but you may be able to make that work for you. Plus, if they do give you the chance to pitch to them, we're golden."

"But if they've shot all your other guys down, why wouldn't they do the same to me?"

"Because of Dubai, Jake. You can walk into a room the equivalent of a minefield and walk out unscathed with the keys to the kingdom in your hand."

He appreciated the compliment, but it still didn't make sense. Why would a billionaire developer want this small piece of land?

Jake ran his hand through his hair. "So, you want me to convince a couple of old people to sell a scrap of land? But there's got to be plenty of open real estate in that area. If you want property on the New England coastline, there are many more choices. Especially ones not as remote as Woolwich Cove."

Charlie leaned in, gaze darkening. "I don't think you're hearing me, Jake. I want *this* land. And you've been with me long enough to know that I get what I want. Don't mistake for a moment that because I'm in the AARP crowd that I've lost my edge. Let's up the ante. How about I sweeten the deal? You get me Camp Woolwich, and I'll make you a full partner. Do you know what that means?"

He sure as hell did.

Charlie ran Linton Holdings himself. There were no partners. Just Charles P. Linton, reigning supreme at the top of his empire. To become a full partner meant Linton Holdings would one day be his to control.

Jake Teller, the boy orphaned at thirteen who scraped his way through life, beating out others with higher pedigrees and unlimited resources, would control it all.

And more than money or sex or the thrill of closing a deal, the thing Jake craved most was control.

If convincing a couple to sell a few hundred acres of land in Maine was the price, then he'd suck it up, ignore the wounds of his past, and write the damn check himself.

It was time to lock away the memories and do what he did best.

"How high are you willing to go?" he asked his mentor.

Charlie's hint of a smile was back. "Twenty-five. Thirty, tops. If you can scoop it up for twenty, I'll give you the damn five as a partner bonus."

Five million.

Sure, he had almost ten million sacked away, but to make a cool five with one deal was nothing to scoff at.

Charlie leaned in. "But you can't mention Linton Holdings. This deal will need to be transacted under one of our subsidiaries. Use Lighthouse Investments if anyone asks."

Jake frowned. "Is this that delicate of a deal?"

It wasn't that uncommon for developers to remain anonymous, but that was usually for high-profile or controversial projects.

Charlie narrowed his gaze. "Think of what you want, Jake. Think of what closing this deal will mean."

It would mean everything. An everything that might be able to fill the void in his heart.

He swallowed past the lump in his throat. "I'll do it."

His boss looked past him and nodded, a damn strange thing to do after offering up his company. But when Jake turned and found a man in a dark suit sporting a chauffeur's cap heading their way, he shook his head.

"You old bastard! How'd you know I'd say yes?"

"Because you're hungry, Jake, and you're willing to do whatever it takes to get to the top. I know a thing or two about that," Charlie replied, then waved the driver over.

The man nodded to Charlie. "Good afternoon, Mr. Linton. Mr. Teller, I picked up your bags from your suite and took the liberty to pack the additional items Mr. Linton had sent over from the Bergen Mountain Sports store in Denver."

"Mountain sports store?" Jake questioned.

Charlie gave him a dry laugh. "You've been to Maine, Jake. We can't have you trouncing around in five-thousand-dollar suits. I know the Bergen family and asked them to pull together some apparel for the trip."

"I could have stopped by my place."

While Linton Holding was a global company with offices all over the world, the headquarters were located in Denver. He had a loft downtown, a place he rarely saw the inside of thanks to all the time he'd spent traveling to procure and oversee the Linton properties. But he could have picked up what he needed. He had the right gear. You didn't get abs like his parked in a conference room. He was an accomplished climber and could knock out a six-minute mile in his sleep.

Charlie glanced at his watch. "There's no time. The next flight to Portland leaves in an hour."

"You're not fucking around on the timeline for this, are you?" he joked, but Charlie didn't crack a smile.

"I've waited a long time to get this land, and if you hadn't noticed, time isn't something I have in spades."

Jake held his mentor's gaze. "Are you all right? Is there anything I need to know?"

Charlie waved him off. "I'll be better when the deed to Woolwich Cove is in my hands," he said, then glanced over at the blonde, still lingering in the auditorium. "I'll take care of your friend over there, Jake. All your tall, dark, and handsome may work with the ladies, and I might not be as strapping as I was fifty years ago, but I'd be willing to bet that the nine zeros on my bank statement can seal the deal with that sweet piece of ass."

Charlie had never married, so it wasn't too out of the ordinary for him to go after an attractive woman, but something was off.

"You're not a betting man, Charlie. You're the one who taught me how to see it all in black and white and filter out the bullshit shades of gray."

A muscle ticked in his mentor's jaw. "Take in the Maine air. Eat some goddamn lobster. Buy a boat and sail the coast."

"I don't do boats," Jake shot back, his voice void of emotion.

Charlie rested a hand on his shoulder and lowered his voice. "Then forget the boats and do however many blondes you like while you're in Maine but get me that land."

Jake tried to discern what was lurking behind his boss's hazel gaze when Charlie gave him one last slap to the shoulder, then sauntered down the row toward the woman with the killer cleavage.

"Shall we?" the driver offered and gestured to the exit.

Jake stared at the door and steadied himself. Ready or not, he was going back to Maine.

3

JAKE

Jake settled himself into the town car and tried to relax into the plush leather seat as the vehicle merged into traffic. He needed to quiet his mind and get focused, but his thoughts churned and whirled as fragments of his childhood accosted his mind.

Maybe it was the fact that he was heading to Camp Woolwich or the oddity of Charlie offering to make him a partner if he were able to procure a tiny parcel of land. His mentor had built luxury resorts in remote areas before, but he'd stuck to purchasing properties in warmer climates where the place wasn't packed in ice and frigid temperatures for a decent chunk of the year.

Then it hit him. That Dubai transaction may have put him on the fast-track at Linton, but if this Maine deal went through, he'd be set—totally and completely in control.

He'd relied on himself for the better part of his life.

No safety net.

No family there to catch him if he fell.

He leaned his head against the seat and inhaled, smelling the sea air as if he were already back at Camp

Woolwich. As if a moment hadn't passed since his mystery girl entered his life that night when he was sent to meet his kiss keeper. She was everywhere. Her soft lips. Her graceful neck. His hands on her shoulders. The way he could hear the smile in her voice—that gentle warmth woven in with the honeyed scent of blackberries. His first impression of her had been sightless, and even when he'd gotten a glimpse, she was still shrouded in darkness with that damned bandana. So, he'd relied on his other senses to paint a picture of her in his mind.

A faceless masterpiece held together by touch, scent, taste, and sound.

"Sir, we've arrived."

Jake blinked open his eyes. Jesus! He could not allow thoughts of some thirteen-year-old mystery girl to derail the importance of closing this deal. He caught his reflection in the window and smoothed his jacket.

With a body that rivaled most fitness gurus, he wasn't some gangly thirteen-year-old anymore. And he sure as hell couldn't let that kid wreck this opportunity.

Time to get his head in the game. He could pull property records and research the Woolwich family on his flight. Hell, by this time tomorrow, he could be ordering new business cards with the title *partner* printed prominently under his name.

The driver removed his bag from the trunk and handed him his boarding pass. Jake slipped the man a twenty, then headed inside to catch his flight.

The line for TSA screening was insane, and he was grateful he didn't have to wait with the herds of unseasoned travelers. Usually, void of Hawaiian shirt-wearing idiots and screaming toddlers, the exclusive PreCheck security line, and the ability to fly First Class were the only ways to maintain one's sanity when navigating the world of commercial air travel. He headed to the familiar spot, then froze to find the area empty.

This was not good.

He blew out a breath and spied a familiar face. Thanks to spending a decent amount of time in the Denver airport, Jake was on friendly terms with many of the security agents and recognized the man staffing the empty area.

"What's going on, Tim?"

The TSA agent shrugged. "System's down. Everyone has to go through the main line today."

"Shit," Jake murmured.

"It might not be so bad. I wouldn't mind being stuck in line behind her," the man replied, gesturing with his chin toward a woman at the end of the line.

Dressed in a trench coat and red heels, the stunning brunette stood in line, her gaze bouncing wildly between her phone and the airport's bustling main lobby like a sexed-up bobblehead doll.

"I don't know. She looks a little...off-balance," he answered.

"I'll take off-balance any day of the week. The crazy ones are always great in the sack," the man joked, but Jake didn't laugh.

For once in his life, he had no interest in bedding a woman—crazy or otherwise. He had too much on his mind. He bid the agent goodbye, then got in line behind the twitchy lady.

"No, no, no, no! Not the curse!" she murmured, staring at her phone, confirming his initial assessment of her above-average level of craziness when she caught his eye.

She blinked back tears. "Could you do something for me, sir?"

Dammit! Why did the crazy ones always ask for help?

"What do you need help with?" he asked as unhelpfully as possible.

"I think my boyfriend just dumped me over text," she blurted.

His brows knit together. "You *think* you just got dumped?"

She shook her head, then held out her phone with a string of texts illuminated on the screen.

This isn't working for me. Have a good life.

"Jesus, that's harsh," he said. Even he wasn't that big of a dick.

The woman swallowed back tears. "He's here. I know he's here because he did that check-in thing on his social media accounts to notify everyone that he'd landed at the Denver airport. I thought, maybe if I could see him, if we talked, he might change his mind. We're supposed to go on a trip together today."

"What do you want me to do?" he asked.

She was back on her cell, scrolling through pictures now, then held up her phone. Instead of her text feed, an image of a man appeared on the screen.

"This is him. It's the only picture I have. He doesn't like his face splashed all over the internet. Can you look around and try to spot him?"

Active enough online to post his location but unable to take a pic with his girlfriend?

That wasn't a good sign for this chick.

Not to mention that the Denver airport is the fifth busiest in the US. Finding one guy in the masses was like looking for a needle in a haystack. He was about to tell this to his crazy line lady when he glanced into the lobby and did a double take. The same SOB in the photo she'd shown him was right there, crossing the length of the area where the newly arrived passengers congregated.

He craned his head. "I think I see him."

She gasped. "Where is he?"

"He's behind you, but don't turn around."

"Why not?" she asked.

Jake flicked his gaze from the man to his crazy line lady, then back to the man. "Let me watch him for a second."

"I'll text him, and you can tell me what he does," she added with a burst of energy.

He released an impatient sigh. What the hell was wrong with him? The last thing he needed was to get in the middle of a breakup, but when the crazy line lady pegged him with her emerald eyes, he couldn't look away.

"Please! This is a big day, and I need him with me. I could really use your help," she pleaded.

"Text him," he grumbled.

Better to get this shit over with quickly.

Clicks peppered the air as the woman went to town, typing out a message.

She met his gaze. "Okay, I sent it."

He watched as the boyfriend glanced at his phone, then pocketed it.

"I don't know if he got it?"

"Oh, crap! A text just came in from my mom. Maybe that messed it up. Let me text her, and then I'll send him another."

She was back at it, texting like a tween on a sugar high.

"Okay, I responded to my mom, and I sent my boyfriend the second text," she replied breathlessly.

He spied the boyfriend and...shit!

The guy wasn't responding to the texts because he was with another woman. A damn attractive woman.

"Well, what's happening?" she asked with those expectant eyes.

"He's saying hello to some woman," Jake answered, choosing his words carefully.

The crazy line lady nodded. "That's all right. He travels a bunch for work. There's a good chance he could run into a colleague at the airport."

Jake observed as the boyfriend proceeded to not only lay a kiss on this *colleague* but grab a handful of her ass as they engaged in some major airport PDA.

He slid his gaze from the exhibitionists to his crazy line lady, surprised by how much it pained him to have to break the news to her. Why the hell should he care if she got dumped? She was no one to him.

He schooled his features. "I'm pretty sure he's not your boyfriend anymore."

"What?" she whispered in a wretched squeak, then spun around in time to see the boyfriend lift the other woman into his arms, press her back to a pillar and start dry-humping next to a sign directing passengers not to leave their baggage unattended.

She held her phone to her chest. "Oh my, God! I got dumped, and I lost my job on the same day."

"And you're holding up the line. Move it, sister!" called an angry voice from behind.

His crazy line lady stared up at him, her mouth opening and closing like a fish out of water.

He should ignore her. He should pop in his earbuds and pretend that he had to take a call. But for whatever reason, he couldn't.

"Is that yours?" he asked, gesturing to a large bag slumped on the ground.

"Yeah," she answered in a daze.

He picked up the heavy canvas tote and set it on top of his roller bag. "Come on. We need to move forward."

She nodded and followed him like a sleepwalker.

What the hell was he supposed to say to this newly dumped and recently unemployed crazy lady now? He was probably the least qualified person in the entire airport to counsel someone on devastating life events. Thank Christ, she didn't say much as they wove their way through the security line.

They handed their tickets to the TSA agent and were funneled into a screening line when she gripped his arm and pointed to a woman ahead of them.

"Why is that lady taking off her jacket?" she asked, panic lacing her words.

He glanced down at her. "TSA rules. Coats and bulky clothing can set off the scanner."

She pulled the trench tighter around her chest. "I can't take off this coat!"

"Why not?"

She waved him down. "I'm only wearing lingerie underneath it."

Now that was a damn surprise. He reared back, and his face must have registered his amazement because his crazy line lady gasped.

She pressed her hands to her hips and frowned. "Do I not seem like the type of woman to do that? Do I not strike you as someone who is sexually adventurous?"

Holy hell! This was getting into some dangerous territory, and he didn't even know this woman's name.

"Honestly?" he sputtered.

With fire in her eyes, she cocked her head to the side. "Yes, honestly!"

"No, you seem like the exact opposite of that kind of

woman. You seem more like a leggings and a baggy sweater kind of person. The lingerie under a trench is a nice move—don't get me wrong—but one best done on a private plane without the possibility of going through a pat-down."

She covered her face with her hands. "What are we going to do?"

We?

How had they become a *we* in less than fifteen minutes?

He glanced at the agents. "We'll play it cool. I travel a decent amount, and I recognize one of the guys working. Let me try to talk to him."

Relief softened her expression, and she smiled so sweetly that he nearly bent down and kissed her plump lips.

"Ma'am, you need to remove your jacket to go through the scanner."

Their moment disintegrated at the sound of the TSA agent's voice, and his crazy line lady stiffened.

"I can't. This isn't a jacket. It's...a dress."

"It looks like a jacket," the agent shot back.

"Nope, it's a dress," she repeated nervously.

"Hey, Benny," he said, extending his hand and praying his crazy line lady came off as someone uneasy about flying instead of a complete nutcase.

The agent's annoyed demeanor dialed down a notch as they shook hands. "Jake Teller, how are you doing, man?"

"Your name is Jake?" his crazy line lady exclaimed, gripping the sleeve of his suit and staring at him like she was... well, pretty damn crazy.

"You know this lady, Jake?" the agent asked.

Jake leaned in toward her like he was going to kiss her but stopped a breath short of his lips touching her earlobe. "Air travel 101: Don't act crazy," he whispered.

She gave a minute nod and tightened her grip on his arm.

He slapped on his slickest smile. "Yeah, we're together. This is a game we play, right?"

His crazy line lady nodded. "Yeah, I date a lot of Jakes, so it's an inside joke between us, right...Jake?"

The agent eyed her skeptically. "How many Jakes have you dated in your life, lady?"

Jake was thinking the same damn thing.

"Counting him?" she asked, dead serious.

"Yeah, counting him," the agent answered with a hint of amusement, which was damn better than suspicion when interacting with a government security official.

She glanced up, her thumb making tiny nervous circles against his skin. "Well...he's number seven," she answered, holding his gaze as a strange déjà vu vibe seemed to pass between them.

"Lucky number seven," the agent laughed, interrupting their peculiar moment.

"All right. You can go through in your *dress*," the man said, waving her into the scanner's chamber.

Jake set their bags on the conveyer belt and followed her. Thank God she didn't have an Uzi or a ten-gallon jug of bleach in her heavy as fuck carry-on. They picked up their items, and he was ready to part ways when her hand was back on his forearm.

"Let me buy you a drink or a snack or something to thank you for your help. You've been the brightest part to literally one of the worst days of my life," she said with that damn sweet smile.

He stared at her. He hadn't really looked at her yet.

"Did you cut yourself? You've got a red mark on your cheek," he asked.

Her hand flew to her face. "It's probably a little paint. I am...I mean, I was an elementary school art teacher."

She'd brushed at her cheek but missed the spot. Without thinking, he stroked his thumb over the pale streak on the apple of her cheek, and the red bit of paint flaked away, and time stopped.

They stood there, staring at each other while travelers veered around them as if a protective bubble surrounded them, and again, he felt the urge to kiss her. She bit down on her lip, and her inadvertent sultry move diverted his blood supply south to his cock. He took a lock of her hair and twisted it around his finger, mesmerized by this stranger when a baby wailed nearby, and the bubble popped. He released the lock of chestnut hair as his blood supply rerouted back to his brain. He was not one of those idiots who could get so wrapped up in a woman that he'd block traffic in the middle of an airport. He dropped his hand from her cheek to rest on her shoulder, and his thumb brushed her collarbone.

"Oh!" she gasped, staring at him as if she recognized him when the last call for his flight to Portland rang out over the intercom.

He glanced past her. "That's my flight."

Her eyes went wide. "That's my flight!"

He shook his head. Fucking hell!

"Come on! We have to run. Give me your bag."

She reared back. "Are you going to try to steal it?"

He threw up his hands. "I just got you past TSA. We're in a completely secure building. Where the hell do you think I'm going to go with your bag?"

"If you tried to steal my bag, it's not like I could chase you. I can't run in heels. I'm not really a stiletto girl," she added, staring down at her sexy as hell and as impractical as fuck footwear.

"Christ," he bit out, dreading what he had to do.

Before she could stop him, he scooped her up into his arms and slung her over his shoulder.

"What are you doing?" she shrieked.

"Getting us on that plane," he said, grabbing their bags and setting off toward the gate.

"Like this? Carrying me, like a sack of potatoes?"

"I can't be the first Jake that's done this to you. You've dated seven of us."

She pounded her fists against his back. "I've dated six Jakes. And I wouldn't call what we're doing as dating. This is more like manhandling."

The gate came into sight, and he switched from a jog to a full sprint. "Congratulations, you can now say you've been manhandled by a Jake. Just add it to your Jake list."

But she'd stopped wiggling.

"Are you okay, Heels?" he asked.

"Are we going to make it? My family already thinks I'm a flighty idiot who can't keep a job. Oh, Jake, I can't miss this plane!" she cried, her voice bobbling as she jostled with each of his strides.

He couldn't miss the plane either. He had five million reasons to get to Maine.

"Hold the door, your last two passengers are here," he called to the gate agent.

The woman glanced down at an iPad. "Passengers Teller and Callahan?"

He patted her thigh. "Is that you, Heels? You're Callahan?"

"Yes, Natalie Callahan. That's me," she answered, from somewhere near his lumbar spine.

He stopped in front of the gate agent and handed her his ticket.

The woman raised an eyebrow. "Do you mind putting your girlfriend down, sir?"

"Yeah, Jake, I'm good to walk the jet bridge on my own, and I'm getting a little woozy with all the upside-down running."

He stared down at the dangling red stilettos—a stark reminder that he had an actual person slung over his shoulder.

"Sorry," he stammered and removed the woman from his body.

The agent took their tickets. "All right, you two, go! The pilot is not going to be happy if we keep the plane waiting any longer."

"Lead the way, Heels," he said and followed half a step behind his crazy line lady who had a name.

Natalie Callahan.

It suited her—the lightness of it. It made him think of the sun peeking in from the blinds, cutting through the darkness.

He pushed the pussy-poetic musing out of his head and ran his hand down the scruff of his jaw. After that mad dash, he needed a stiff drink and a few hours of quiet.

"Welcome to First Class, Miss Callahan. You're in seat 3B."

He glanced at his ticket.

2A. Thank you, Universe!

At least he wasn't going to be stuck sitting next to her. He stowed his bag, then settled himself in the window seat next to an older gentleman.

He nodded to the man, and the man nodded back, and relief washed over him. That minute exchange was international man language for *I won't bother you if you don't bother me.*

This gentleman was most likely another business traveler who'd know better than to engage in a round of twenty questions. Jake sat back, closed his eyes, so ready to just breathe for a damn second when a woman's voice cut through the hum of conversations buzzing inside the plane.

"Gary, this lovely young woman said she wouldn't mind switching seats so we can sit together."

Jake opened his eyes to find his crazy line lady standing in the aisle.

Jesus! He could not catch a break. Come on, karma. He'd helped her get through security and catch a flight! Now, all he wanted was some damn downtime to work.

Natalie sat down next to him, all smiles.

"I've never flown First Class," she said as the flight attendant handed them each a flute of champagne.

He glanced at his new seatmate. "I'm going to need a Jameson on the rocks. Make it a double."

Natalie downed her glass then gestured to his. "Do you want it?"

He shook his head, and she polished off his champagne in no time flat.

Perfect! He was seated next to a newly dumped, recently unemployed alcoholic.

"You may want to go easy on the bubbles," he offered.

He had to get her out of his head. That paint on the cheek bullshit and their googly-eyed antics could not happen again.

She gave him a weak smile. "I'm a little nervous. I thought it might take the edge off."

The flight attendant handed him his drink, then refilled both champagne flutes.

Natalie polished off both before he'd even taken one sip of his whiskey.

"I'm not a big drinker," she said with a hiccup.

He closed his eyes. "You could have fooled me."

She released an audible breath. "So, why are you going to Maine?"

Here we go. Twenty questions.

He never talked business on a plane. Over the years, he'd gotten many tips, listening in on so-called professionals, clucking loudly about financial troubles or upcoming shifts in the market. Nope, he kept his damn mouth shut.

"A little recreation and some peace and quiet," he added, hoping she'd take the hint.

She didn't.

"My grandparents live in Maine. It's their fiftieth wedding anniversary. They're having the whole family fly in for it. And my family is pretty big and can be a little overwhelming, like the Kennedys."

He cocked his head to the side. "Your family's in politics?"

"No," she answered with a shake of her head.

"You're Irish Catholic?"

"Nope," she said as the flight attendant refilled the glasses.

"So, your family is nothing like the Kennedys," he challenged.

She downed a glass. "It's a big family," she replied as her cheeks grew pink from the champagne.

"Sounds like fun," he answered dryly.

"Where are you staying?" she pressed.

"I'm not sure. I'm playing it by ear."

That was the truth. He hadn't even looked into lodging. His security line capers with Heels over here had deprived him of all rational thought for the past half hour. He was about to connect to the plane's Wi-Fi and get on that when his seatmate tapped on the television screen embedded in the seat in front of her like a toddler.

"This is some tricky stuff," she said with a slight slur.

There's the bubbly kicking in.

"Put on your seatbelt, Heels. They don't let you watch TV during the safety demo."

She crossed her legs and gazed at her footwear. "I thought I could be that girl. I thought that's what he wanted," she mused, the ache in her voice near palpable.

Fucking Jake number six! He cursed the douche who shared his name. Thanks to him dumping his girlfriend, now he—Jake the seventh—was stuck picking up the pieces.

"Sit back," he said, then fastened her belt for her as she ran her finger down the spike of her heel.

The flight attendant began the safety demonstration as the plane taxied to the runway, and despite knocking back nearly an entire bottle of champagne, his crazy line lady paid attention.

Probably the teacher in her.

He mentally punched himself. She means nothing. She's some lady having a shit day. Some lady who looked stunning in a trench, and, despite not being able to run in heels, she wore the hell out of them.

Natalie remained quiet through the safety demo and didn't say a word as the plane took off and hit its cruising altitude. He almost thought he was in the clear when she turned to him, all shining emerald eyes and a trembling bottom lip.

"You're a good person, for a Jake," she said then hiccupped.

He handed her a napkin, and she dabbed at her eyes.

"Sorry, I get a little tipsy and emotional with champagne and tequila and rum and wine. Jake number two from college would always say—"

"Let me guess, that you're a lightweight," he finished.

Her face lit up. "Yes, that's exactly what he said."

"Maybe you should steer clear of Jakes," he offered.

She leaned in. "You're not so bad."

He wanted to tell her he was bad, probably one of the worst Jakes out there. He only cared about making money. But he couldn't get the damn words out.

She drummed her fingers on the armrest. "Maybe you're right. Maybe I should give up Jakes. In all the years of dating them, not one ever put me first. And come to think of it, they were all pretty awful in the end."

"There you go," he replied.

"And do you know what else I need to steer clear of, Jake number seven?" she asked, all earnest eyes and kissable lips.

He shook his head.

"My witch cousins and their toe obsessed perverted husbands."

He reared back. "Your what?"

She sunk into the seat. "Leslie and Lara and their husbands. They're awful, and they're all podiatrists."

He didn't know any podiatrists but couldn't imagine that all of them were awful.

"Are they bad doctors?" he asked, needing some clarification.

"No, my cousins have teased and tormented me for ages, and now that they're married, their husbands try to find ways to touch my feet."

He cringed. "That's damn creepy, even if they are podiatrists."

"Right," she answered, nearly knocking over the empty champagne flutes.

He handed them to the flight attendant as Natalie pulled a face mask from their first-class complimentary box.

She held it out for him.

"No thanks," he said, and she frowned the cutest damn frown he'd ever seen.

"No, silly! It's for me. Can you take it out of the plastic wrapper? I can't feel the tip of my nose anymore."

He bit back a grin. "You don't open it with your nose," he replied, staring into her sparkling green eyes—now considerably more sparkly from the champagne.

"I think I need a nap," she said, fanning herself as her cheeks grew rosier.

He ripped open the plastic and removed the sleep mask. He went to hand it to her, but she closed her eyes, then leaned forward.

"Can you put it on me? I don't want to get it all caught in my hair."

She had beautiful hair. Long and dark. It brushed past her shoulders in subtle waves. He could still feel the strand wrapped around his finger.

Jake Number Seven, stop!

He threw another mental punch at his brain. He was not Jake number seven. He would not be Jake number anything to anybody.

He pulled the mask over her head, careful not to mess up her hair, then pulled the material over her eyes and...

And he stared at her. With the mask in place and half her face covered, he couldn't peel his gaze away.

"Am I good?" she asked as that weird déjà vu sensation took hold again.

"Yeah, you're good," he answered as she leaned back.

She sighed. "Do you have a pillow?"

He glanced around. No dice. "I can ask the flight attendant for one when he passes by."

"That's okay," she yawned and rested her head on his shoulder.

He didn't move. He only listened as her breaths grew slow and even as she drifted off to sleep, and surprisingly, he relaxed. It was only then that he realized how tense he'd been since he'd agreed to Charlie's proposition.

He glanced at his slumbering, possibly champagne addicted seatmate, then carefully picked up his glass of Jameson and sipped the smooth spirit. But just as he set his glass down, Natalie swayed forward, and he caught her and brought her back to him.

Fuck it!

He wrapped his arm around her, and she nuzzled into him.

"Thanks, Jake," she said in a sleepy sigh.

Which Jake? He could almost laugh. There were seven to choose from, right? He stared down at the giant mask covering her face, then closed his eyes, and tilted his head to rest against hers.

He could always go back to being an asshole when they landed.

4

Half-awake, Natalie twisted what she thought was a bedsheet around her hand, melting into the warmth around her until a tap at her shoulder pulled her out of that cozy space sandwiched between sleep and wakefulness.

She opened her eyes only to find complete darkness, then remembered the sleep mask. She peeled up the fabric covering one eye and was met with the smiling face of their First-Class flight attendant.

"You two look so cute. I hate to have to wake you."

Slightly disoriented, thanks to all that champagne, Nat pushed the mask to her forehead. "Where are we?"

Her warm pillow shifted as a hand now rested on her breast.

She was not in bed with Jake number six back in Denver. She was cozied up to a completely different Jake on her flight to Portland.

The safe, comfy feeling disintegrated.

She'd made it, and now she'd have to contend with her cousins—all by herself.

She tried to edge her way out of Jake's embrace, but

underneath that suit, the man had some serious muscles, and she couldn't get him to budge.

Nat glanced around. There wasn't a passenger in sight. "Where is everyone?"

"They've all deplaned," the man answered.

"Oh! Wow."

It was pretty creepy being the last one on a plane.

"I'll give you a minute," he said and headed toward the flight crew assembled near the front of the aircraft.

She released the handful of Jake's shirt, then closed her eyes and listened to the soothing rise and fall of his breath. Another few seconds couldn't hurt. She'd always craved this kind of closeness, and Jake number six was not a cuddler. Actually, neither were Jakes one through five. She let the memory of the Jakes of her past fade away and inhaled this Jake's clean scent of soap with a hint of sage.

With her head nestled in the crook of his neck, she couldn't see his face, so she reached up and ran her fingertips down his jawline. He hummed a satisfied little sound that sent a warmth emanating through her chest.

"Jake, we've landed in Portland. It's time to wake up," she said and stroked his cheek.

"Hmm," he replied. But her plan to ease him out of slumber got cut short when the flight attendant, now joined by the pilot, the co-pilot, and two other flight attendants crowded in around them.

Trapped in one hell of a bear hug, she smiled up at the flight crew, then switched from a gentle stroke to a *wake-the-hell-up* slap.

He turned his cheek and tightened his grip. Holy Mary! Was this man half boa constrictor?

"Jake, seriously, they need us to get off the plane."

"Plane?" he mumbled, stroking his thumb across her breast.

"Yeah, and you're feeling me up in front of the flight crew."

"What?" he exclaimed, releasing his grip and looking back and forth as if he'd woken up on an alien planet.

Natalie nodded to the flight crew. "Would you mind giving us another minute? I promise that we'll be off in a jiffy."

Jake ran his hands down his face. "I don't usually sleep well. I must have conked out."

She gestured toward the front of the plane where the friendly-skies flight crew looked considerably less friendly. "We better go. I think we're holding them up."

Jake nodded, then made an awkward gesture toward her breasts. "Sorry about that."

She stood in the aisle and waved him off. "No worries. You were asleep, right?"

He joined her in the aisle and removed their bags from the bin above their seats. "You think I felt you up on purpose?"

"No, I didn't mean that. I meant that it was probably an accident," she tossed back.

He held her gaze. "Heels, if I were to feel you up on purpose, you'd know it."

Heels.

Not counting Nat, Nat the little brat—a gem her cousins cooked up—she'd never had a nickname.

"So, you think you're super awesome with the ladies?" she challenged.

He shrugged, and she laughed.

"Men."

"You mean Jakes, in your case. It's probably a good thing you've given them up," he added with a sly smile.

He had her there—the jackass.

But he wasn't a jackass. He'd gotten her through security, and he'd stuck by her while she watched her boyfriend suck face with some random woman.

And then it hit her.

She'd told everyone she was bringing a date—bringing Jake. Natalie Callahan, the loser in love and life, had emailed her entire family that, for the first time ever at a Woolwich family event, she would be accompanied by someone who thought the sun rose and set with her smile.

Oh, God! She'd used those exact words, too.

Her stomach clenched as she imagined Lara and Leslie's smug faces when she arrived, boyfriendless.

Jake pressed his hand to her lower back, jolting her from her doomsday scenario. "Are you all right?"

She shook off the impending disaster. "Yeah."

He leaned in. "Do you need to throw up? You look a little green."

"No, I'm thinking of my family," she answered as they exited the plane and walked across the jet bridge to the terminal.

"The perverts?" he asked.

"The what?" she exclaimed as they continued down the concourse.

"The podiatrists. On the plane, you said they were perverts."

She hung her head, recalling her tipsy tirade. "My stupid champagne mouth."

"You did knock back a few."

Or five.

They continued on in silence. And she glanced around the familiar airport. In a week, she'd be back here, most likely with a bruised ego and another chunk of her self-esteem whittled away by her witch cousins. But she'd make it.

How much could happen in a week?

She could hide out in her cabin or sneak away to do art projects with all the great-grandkids. And she loved Camp Woolwich as much as she loved her grandparents. They'd never jumped on the Natalie bashing bandwagon. They had to have known about all of her misfortunes—all her lost jobs and failed relationships—but they'd never mentioned it.

And she knew she'd always hold a special place in their hearts.

She was their youngest grandchild, and that had meant extra time with them when she was little. While the older kids ran off to play capture the flag and paddle canoes over to their small island, she'd stay close to her grandparents, waving to her cousins from her grandpa's arms.

Unfortunately, she wasn't four years old anymore. And with all their friends and family coming in for the fiftieth-anniversary celebration, it may be a stretch to find a single quiet moment with them.

"How about I walk you to baggage claim and then..." Jake began, breaking into her thoughts.

And then, he'd be just another Jake who'd passed through her revolving door of Jakes. But even though she'd decided to give up Jakes, she wasn't ready to say goodbye to this one quite yet.

"Do you want to grab something to eat? I still owe you for helping me," she asked, trying not to sound too pathetic.

A muscle ticked in his jaw. "I should be going."

"So soon?" she asked, then winced.

Her stupid mouth! Now she looked desperate, but she didn't need to lay it out there like a Sunday picnic.

"We've been together for the last five hours," he replied.

"But we were unconscious for four of them," she parried back, trying to be funny.

She should not try to be funny.

"Heels, I'm not a Jake that you want to add to your list."

Anger edged out her embarrassment. "My what?"

"Your list of Jakes—I can't be one of them."

Heat rose to her cheeks. "First of all, I'm done with Jakes. And for the record, I wasn't asking you to be one of them. I was trying to be polite."

"You should stop. That could be why all those Jakes treat you like a doormat," he replied.

She gasped. "A doormat! How dare you! You don't know the first thing about me."

His features hardened. "I know your cheating boyfriend dumped you via text and that you're unemployed."

Dammit! He did know everything. Still, it didn't give him the right to judge her.

She took a step forward, grabbed his tie, and pulled him down to meet her eye to eye. Their breaths met in the millimeters between them, and a shiver ran down her spine. A delicious tingling that made her want to close her eyes and pull him in that fraction closer where their lips could meet.

She steadied herself. "There's a lot more to me than that. I'm—"

"Natalie, is that you?"

Like nails on a chalkboard, Leslie's voice rang out.

"Shit," she whispered, holding Jake's gaze.

"This must be the Jake of the hour," her cousin added.

"Which one? There are like twenty of them." Lara giggled, still piggybacking off her sister like they were kids.

Natalie swallowed hard. She couldn't go back to Camp Woolwich, a complete failure with no job and no boyfriend. For once, she wanted her family to at least think that she had it together.

"You have to help me, Jake," she whispered.

He frowned. "Help you how?"

She flicked her gaze to her cousins, standing with their husbands. Unsurprisingly, both men's eyes were locked on her feet.

"Be my last Jake for one week," she whispered, hoping he could see the desperation written all over her face.

"Your last Jake?" he threw back, eyebrows nearly hitting his hairline.

"Now, don't be so selfish and keep him all to yourself, Nat. Introduce us."

She took a step back and glanced at the women. With matching bob haircuts and sensible shoes, it had been a few years since she'd seen them in person. But when it came to her least favorite family members, absence didn't make the heart grow fonder.

"Jake, these are my cousins, Leslie and Lar—"

Leslie cleared her throat. "Natalie, you're forgetting something," Les said with a condescending smirk.

Natalie plastered on a grin. It would take everything she had to make it through this week.

"Jake, these are my cousins, Dr. Leslie Dixtown, Dr. Lara Dixtown, and their husbands, Dr. Leo Dixtown and Dr. Marcus Dixtown."

"*Dicks town*?" Jake repeated slowly.

"*Dix-ton*," Les corrected, repeating the two syllables at light-speed. "It's meant to be spoken quickly."

"*D-I-X-T-O-N?*" Jake spelled out.

"*D-I-X-T-O-W-N.* The *W* is silent," Les threw back.

Dammit! She'd forgotten the silent *W.*

"Or you can shorten it to Doctor Dix. That's what our patients call us," Lara's idiot husband chirped.

"I bet they do," Jake murmured under his breath.

"And this Dr. Dix doesn't approve of that kind of footwear for air travel," Leo, Leslie's husband, said, while his brother went back to staring at her stilettos as if they were covered in chocolate.

Ugh! These guys were the worst. If she weren't basically naked, she'd whip off her trench coat and sling it over her heels to stop the freaks from feasting on her footsies.

Nat glanced at Jake to find him frowning as he watched Lara and Leslie's husbands' eye-hump her feet.

But she had no time to worry about the Dix brothers. She had to act fast. This was her last chance to recruit back up.

"Look! The bags are loading onto the carousel! Come on, Jake. You can help me get it while the others wait here," she blurted, grabbing his hand and pulling him toward the baggage claim area.

"Holy hell, Heels! Those people are..."

"A bunch of dicks?" she offered.

His stoic demeanor cracked and gave way to the hint of a smile.

She released a tight breath. It was now or never.

"You said you didn't have any set plans. No hotel. Nothing scheduled, right?"

He nodded.

"Come with me. My grandparents have plenty of room at their place. You'd only have to hang out with us for a few meals, and then you could do your own thing the rest of the time. If you can't already tell, I need one last Jake in my life. Will you be my fake Jake for a week?"

His gaze slid past her. "Natalie, for all you know, I'm a serial killer."

She cupped his cheek in her hand and forced him to meet her eye. "Maybe you're just a part-time serial killer, and this trip to Maine is a respite from all the...carnage."

A frown line pulled between his brows. "Do you hear yourself? You said you'd be fine spending the week with a monster."

"You met my cousins. I'm already going to be surrounded by monsters," she replied, really liking the feel of his scruff on her fingertips.

His gaze dropped to the ground. "This is crazy."

"I know," she whispered back.

They studied each other, and she could feel the rejection coming. It was like her sixth sense. Just when something seemed too good to be true, things got worse. But that didn't stop her from pleading with the universe.

Say yes! Say yes! Say yes! Please, Kiss Keeper Curse, cut a gal some slack.

She channeled all her mental energy into this man when a voice cut off her internal plea.

"Nat! I figured this hot pink bag was yours. It was going around and around on the baggage carousel."

"Fish!" she said with a genuine smile and dropped her hand from Jake's face.

The giant of a man she'd known her entire life lumbered over. A former camper who'd gotten hired on as the grounds' keeper at Camp Woolwich and then went on to drive the camp van, Fish had been a part of Camp Woolwich since the first year it opened.

He wrapped her in a warm embrace, and her frayed nerves calmed at the sight of an old friend.

"How are you?" she asked, happy for the momentary distraction.

The gentle giant of a man patted her back. "I'm doing well. Do you have any more bags? We should hit the road. Camp Woolwich awaits!"

Jake's jaw dropped, but he quickly recovered and muted his expression. "Did you say Camp Woolwich?"

Fish's brows knit together. "Yes, the one and only Camp Woolwich, located on Woolwich Cove."

She watched Jake carefully. "Yeah, my grandparents own it."

"They own it?" Jake repeated.

"They sure do," Fish said, extending his hand to Jake. "You must be Jake. It's good to meet you. Call me, Fish." The man squinted, looking out the window at the airport's passenger drop-off zone, and the wrinkles at the corners of his eyes grew deeper. "I drive the camp van that may be parked illegally out front, so we better hit the road. I'll go tell your cousins."

The man left, and she met Jake's gaze, now clouded with disbelief.

Of course, the guy was gobsmacked. What she'd asked him to do was utterly insane. But that didn't change the fact that she needed a Jake.

She held his gaze, doing her best not to look like a lunatic. "I know this is nuts. I know we barely know each other. I know you—"

"I'll do it," he replied, cutting her off.

She cocked her head to the side. Now, she was gobsmacked.

"You'll do it?"

He swallowed hard as pain flashed in his eyes, then blinked, and the emotion disappeared and was replaced with that stoic expression from when she'd first seen him in the security line.

He nodded, seemingly more to himself than to her. "I'll join you at Camp Woolwich. I'll be your Jake."

Overcome with relief, she grabbed onto the lapels of his jacket, pulled him down, and pressed a kiss to his cheek. "Thank you. I promise I'm not insane."

He smiled down at her. But the emotion didn't reach his eyes.

"Enough PDA, Nat! Let's go!" Leslie called as the Dix brigade followed Fish out of the airport.

She hooked her arm with Jake's and started working out their ruse. "Okay, I haven't said much about Jake number six. Sorry for calling him by his number, but you know what I mean."

Jake the seventh nodded.

"All the Jakes may play to our advantage. It's a little confusing," she added.

"I can imagine," he answered, still a little out of it.

She glanced out the sliding glass doors as everyone piled into the camp van. "Here's the rundown. My grandparents are Hal and Bev Woolwich. I have five uncles. My mom is the only Woolwich daughter. My parents are divorced, and my dad lives in California."

"Will he be coming to the camp?" Jake asked.

She shook her head. "No, my parents aren't a-holes to each other, but they've been divorced since I was young and have led very separate lives. And my mom is on assignment in New Zealand. She's a travel writer and won't be able to attend the celebration."

"Okay," he answered, but he seemed conflicted, which

didn't make much sense. He had no connection to Camp Woolwich. If anyone were to go down for this little masquerade, it would be her.

She stared up at him. "Are you ready?"

A muscle ticked in his jaw. "Yes."

They passed through the glass doors, and Jake loaded their bags into the back of the van.

So far, so good.

She poked her head into the vehicle to find all three bench seats occupied. "Les, why aren't you sitting next to Leo?"

Marcus and Lara sat together on one bench while Leslie and Leo each sat on their own.

"I think it best if you sit by me, Natalie. I should examine your feet after your prolonged high heel exposure," Leo said as if it were totally normal to examine somebody's feet in the back of a van.

Jake joined her, then pinned Leo with his gaze. "I suggest you sit next to your lovely wife, Dr. Dix. You don't need to worry about Natalie's feet anymore."

The man puffed up. "Why is that?"

"Because anyone who even tries to touch her baby toe will have to deal with me," Jake answered, lowering his voice.

"But wearing high heels could worsen bunions or aggravate knee or hip pain," Leo sputtered.

Jake turned to her. "Do you have any of those issues, Heels?"

"Heels?" Leo snapped.

"Yeah, that's what I call her because she looks so damn good in high heels," Jake answered with a sly twist of his lips.

Leo gasped. "But the implications are devastating."

"Well, Heels, are your feet falling apart?" Jake asked, tossing her a little wink.

She shook her head. "Nope."

"Look at that, Dr. Dix, she's fine. Now, kindly take the spot next to your wife so I can sit next to my—"

"Girlfriend," she supplied. "I've been your girlfriend for five months and six days since we met at that happy hour in Denver, Colorado," she added, trying to pack as much information as possible to get Jake number seven up to speed.

Everyone stared at her, except Leslie, who was focused on her phone.

Natalie patted her fake boyfriend's arm. "But, of course, you already know all that."

"Of course," he parroted back, his eyes telling her to take it down a notch.

But she could hardly believe this was happening. This random man, who happened to be smoking hot and dressed to the nines, agreed to this...this...con.

That's what it was. With his help, she'd con her family into thinking she was a normal functioning adult.

Leo took his spot on the bench next to Leslie, who continued hammering out an email, oblivious to the whole foot faceoff as Jake helped her into the van.

Her cousin shoved her phone into her purse, and her expression softened. "How's Grandpa doing, Fish?"

The man glanced over his shoulder nervously, which was quite unlike him. "Good, all good," he answered.

Natalie glanced between her cousin and the man she'd known her entire life. "Is there something—"

"And we're off!" Fish called from the driver's seat, cutting off her question as he maneuvered the grumbly old vehicle into traffic.

"Speaking of *being off*, Natalie. Were you laid off or

completely sacked this time?" Leslie remarked with her sour expression back in place.

"How do you know about that?" Nat asked, then the answer hit her.

The old Woolwich family grapevine.

Leslie pulled out her phone. "Your mom texted Aunt Tish, who talked to her daughter-in-law, you know, Pete's wife, Patty, and she texted my mom who texted me."

Lit only by the light of her cell phone, Natalie could see the smug curve of Leslie's lips.

"Another lost job, Natalie. That sucks for you," Lara added.

"It was actually perfect timing. Natalie's going to start freelancing," Jake said without missing a beat.

"I am?" she asked.

"You are. Remember, you'd mentioned that," he said with a conspiratorial lilt.

"Freelancing? Do you even know what your girlfriend does for a living?" Leslie parried.

The breath caught in Nat's throat. She couldn't be outed as a liar and a fraud already. They hadn't even made it to camp yet.

"She's an art teacher. She can run classes out of community centers, teach during the summer at camps, or cater to homeschoolers. There's a world of possibilities for someone with her skills," he answered as smooth as silk.

Natalie resumed her normal breathing. Jake remembered what she did, and his on-the-fly response wasn't a bad idea at all.

She stared at her fake boyfriend. She'd never considered branching out on her own. But why should she limit herself to only working in schools? Art could be taught anywhere. She'd uncovered her love of drawing and painting at Camp

Woolwich. She'd run the arts and crafts program with her grandmother every summer that she was a counselor at camp.

"Is this true, Nat?" Leslie barked.

"Yeah, thanks to Jake, a lot of things that seemed out of reach, now, don't seem so far off."

"Well, I could never live with that kind of instability," Leslie huffed.

Natalie lifted her chin and schooled her features. "Well, I could never live with smelling feet all day long. So, I guess we'll have to agree to disagree when it comes to the life I choose to live."

Leslie stared at her, wide-eyed, and Natalie froze. Holy hell! Had she shoveled Leslie's shit right back at her? Had she actually stood up for herself? She should be bracing for impact. Leslie was sure to sling another criticism her way, but the thrill of not allowing her witch cousin to bulldoze over her made her giddy over this tiny triumph.

"Whatever," Leslie said and turned her attention back to her phone, like a sullen teenager.

She met Jake's gaze, and in the dim light of an on-coming car, he tucked her hair behind her ear then leaned in. "Nice one, Heels."

Her pulse kicked up, but this time, it wasn't from standing up to her raging bitch of a cousin. Jake's scent and the warmth of his breath were what made the butterflies in her belly erupt into flight. She pulled back and met his gaze in the shadowy light as he rested his hand on her shoulder, and just like in the airport, his thumb brushed past her collarbone.

"Thank you," she whispered, tilting her head as if some tractor beam were pulling them together when his phone pinged an incoming text, and they stilled.

"I should check that," he said as that muted quality took hold of his features.

Jake angled his body away from her to respond to the message, and she sat back in the seat with a sinking feeling. He had a life—a life she wasn't a part of. In her mad dash to school him on pertinent Woolwich family details, she hadn't asked him one thing about himself, besides the part-time serial killer stuff. They could get their stories straight tonight. She sighed and stared out the window. The number of on-coming headlights diminished as Fish exited the highway and set off down the dark country road toward Woolwich Cove.

Day or night, she'd know this drive. The tires hit the gravel road leading up to the Woolwich property, and she couldn't help but smile as the memories flooded back.

S'mores by the fire. Cannonballing off the dock as the crisp bite of the cold water shocked her system. Purple stained fingertips from gorging on wild blackberries. And... a kiss. A kiss that was both a curse and a blessing.

Fish parked the van next to the old shed, and Jake craned his head to look out the window.

"I can't believe I'm here. It's..." he trailed off.

She patted his hand. "Everyone feels this way the first time they see it."

The lights from the dock and boathouse lit the darkened sloping acres of the coastal property in an ethereal glow. Dotted by clusters of trees, cabins, and the main house where her grandparents lived, the shadowy body of water surrounding the camp ebbed and flowed in hypnotizing waves.

"You kids head down to your grandparents' place. Hal and Bev saved you some supper. I'll bring your things to your cabins," Fish said, busying himself with the bags.

"Please tell me that Leo and I are in one of the renovated cabins," Leslie barked.

Fish nodded. "Oh, yes! You three happy couples each have one of the honeymoon cottages."

"Thank God!" Leslie huffed.

The Dixtown quartet headed down the path to the main house, but she and Jake stayed behind.

His head swung back and forth, taking it all in.

"It'll be easier to figure out the lay of the land tomorrow," she said, but he didn't respond.

"This place," he murmured.

"What about it?"

He shook his head. "It's nothing."

The door to the main house opened, and her grandparents waved to them from the porch.

"Come on! Come on! You kids must be starving," her grandma Bev called, waving Lara and Leslie and their husbands inside with a hug and a kiss.

This was it. The moment of truth. She brushed her pinky finger against Jake's hand, and as if they'd been doing this for five months and six days, he laced his fingers with hers.

Morality check. While this wasn't the original Jake she'd told everyone she was bringing, it was a Jake. Hopefully, a non-serial killer Jake who could stand-in for a few family events. She wasn't that full of herself to think that anyone besides her cousins cared all that much about her lackluster life, but she needed this. She needed a good, solid Jake. And by some miracle, the universe seemed to have served him up on a platter.

She gave Jake's hand a gentle squeeze as they ascended the steps to the porch. His jaw set in a hard line, he seemed nervous—which would be totally normal for anyone in his situation—but he was so at ease putting Leo in his place. Maybe it was the whole meeting the grandparents song and dance that had him on edge. Unfortunately, or perhaps, fortunately, there was no time to hem and haw. It was fake relationship go time.

She released a shaky breath. "Grandma and Grandpa, this is Jake."

Her grandmother pulled a pair of glasses from her pocket, slid them on, and eyed her fake boyfriend. The Woolwich matriarch shared a look with her husband then pursed her lips.

"Jake, have we met before?"

5

JAKE

His gaze bounced between Bev and Hal Woolwich. He was really here, and he needed to pull it together—and he needed to do it, lickity-damn-split.

It was as if a winning lottery ticket had landed in his lap, and he could not blow it. Not before he'd even gotten past the front door.

Luckily, he had a plan.

He'd play the part of Natalie's devoted boyfriend. He'd run defense and make damn sure that the Dix cousins didn't give her any shit and that the Dix husbands didn't get anywhere near her feet. He'd be attentive and caring—the type of guy any grandparent would want for their beloved granddaughter. Then, once he was in their good graces, he'd subtly test the waters on the possibility of them parting ways with their land. Without them even knowing it, he'd sell them on the lucrative benefits of cashing out. He'd convinced dozens of sellers that it wasn't the property that mattered, but how their quality of life improved once they had millions in the bank—and he'd never struck out. He'd never had a deal go south, and he wasn't about to start now.

Nope, too much was riding on this, and these were the facts: she needed one last Jake, and he needed a way into Camp Woolwich.

It was a transaction.

A trade.

An arrangement.

Just business.

And, when this deal went through, the Woolwich family would come into some serious money.

He was doing them a favor. He was setting them up for life. He'd worked it out like a game of chess, except in his version, nobody should come out feeling like a loser. That was his magic.

He was the closer. The dealmaker.

He should be walking on cloud nine.

But what he didn't expect was the emotional hurricane that hit him the moment he set foot in Camp Woolwich, and the memories came rushing back.

And then there was Natalie.

What would happen if she found out that he'd been tasked with obtaining the deed to Camp Woolwich even before they'd met? How would she react when she learned that he wasn't helping her out for the sake of being a good guy but was instead taking advantage of her position in the Woolwich family?

He swallowed hard and stared at the couple in front of him. He needed to say something.

Fifteen years had passed, but he would have recognized the Woolwich's anywhere. With piercing blue eyes and still sporting a beard, Hal looked thinner than he'd remembered, but Bev looked nearly the same. When he was a camper, she'd worn her hair in a long dark braid that snaked past her shoulder. With only the addition of a silvery streak woven through, she looked nearly identical as to how he'd remembered her.

But she couldn't have recognized him. He was just a boy back then. He started to tell her she must be mistaken when Natalie piped up.

"This is Jake's first visit to Woolwich Cove," she offered, answering for him with a bright smile.

Bev Woolwich squinted and adjusted her glasses. "I'm sorry, Jake. After hosting thousands of campers over the last fifty years, every face seems to look familiar to me, dear."

"Is this the sunrise and sunset boyfriend?" Hal asked with the hint of a smirk, then released a muffled cough.

Natalie pushed up onto her tiptoes and gave the man a kiss on the cheek. "Oh, Grandpa, don't be like that," she said, then frowned and surveyed the man's face. "Are you feeling all right?"

"Right as rain," the man answered.

"I think that it's quite romantic," Bev said, shifting the attention away from her husband, then surprised him by wrapping her arms around him.

Jake returned the embrace and met his fake girlfriend's eye.

"That's my Jake. Always the romantic," she said with a *just-go-with-it* smile.

Natalie's grandfather took in the trench and heels. "That's an interesting outfit. Let me hang your jacket in the closet."

Oh, shit!

"It's a dress," he and his fake girlfriend blurted out in unison.

The man frowned. "That's a dress?"

Natalie pasted on an amped-up grin. "Boy, I'm hungry!"

Note to self. His fake girlfriend was pretty terrible at the art of deception.

"Of course, you must be starving. Come on in and join your cousins! We've got pizza and beer in the kitchen," Bev said, hooking her arm with Natalie's and leading her into the main house while he hung back and walked next to Hal.

Rustic furniture and the scent of pizza woven in with a fire burning in the fireplace made for a cozy setting. Oil paintings and framed photographs blanketed the walls. He stared at image after image of groups of campers, arms slung around each other until one picture caught his eye, and he froze.

It was...him.

There he was, in black and white, standing with a group of campers. He recalled that day, lining up for the all-camp picture as Hal climbed a ladder to take the photograph.

"You found Nat," the man said, stifling a cough then coming to stand next to him.

"I did?" he asked.

Hal tapped the photo, pointing out a young girl with dark hair. "She's right there. That was her first year as a teen camper. The year our little Nat moved up to be with the big kids."

Jake nodded, unable to speak. He hadn't put it together until this moment.

Of course, she would have attended camp here, and that meant they'd been campers at the same time.

But he couldn't recall meeting her.

He'd kept to himself that summer. Thirteen had been an intense age. He'd grown nearly six inches in one year and woke up bright and early every damn day with morning wood. He didn't hang out with the other teen boys doing arts and crafts or playing pickup basketball. Instead, he'd hiked over to an abandoned lighthouse. Supposedly, the home of the Kiss Keeper legend, but for him, it was a place to think and daydream back when he'd wanted to be a marine biologist or a park ranger. He'd even contemplated opening a camp of his own.

Back when he could afford to have silly, childish dreams before the hard punch of reality hit him square in the gut.

Hal's expression grew pensive. "Our Nat's always had a good heart, a kind heart, an artist's heart like Bev. And, like her grandmother, she can't dole it out in parts. It's all or nothing for these Woolwich women, and I fear she's had it broken a time or two."

He got the not so subtle don't *hurt my granddaughter* hint and nodded solemnly.

What else was he supposed to do? Pretending to be her boyfriend, he was walking a fine line, and he didn't want to say anything too incriminating. He didn't want to insinuate that there was a future for them, while at the same time, he needed her family to believe that there was—at least for this week.

"Hal, sweetheart, let Jake get some pizza," Bev called from the kitchen, saving him from a response.

He followed Natalie's grandfather into the snug space and found everyone congregating around a granite kitchen island. He grabbed a plate and served himself two slices of pepperoni when he noticed his fake girlfriend hadn't started eating.

Here was his first chance to look good in front of the fam.

"Natalie, do you want me to get you a slice of pepperoni?"

The chatter stopped, and his fake girlfriend stared at him, panic welling in her eyes.

"Nat's a vegetarian," Lara said, sharing a look with Leslie.

"How did you not know that after five months and six days of dating?" Leslie asked with a condescending smirk.

He caught Natalie's gaze. "I think it's just been a long day of travel."

"Jet lag can do that," Bev offered kindly, but nobody looked convinced.

Natalie crossed the kitchen and came to his side. "And I might be a vegetarian, but Jake knows that I love to watch him eat meat."

"You like to watch your boyfriend eat meat?" Leo threw back.

Shit! This was going downhill quick.

Marcus raised his hand like a kindergartner. "Meat voyeurism is a thing. People post about it on YouTube. I spent all last weekend watching videos of some chick downing a T-bone."

"Don't mind us, Jake. Meat-eat away," Leslie said with a wave of her hand.

Dammit! Why couldn't he have offered her a slice of cheese?

He picked up the piece of pepperoni and held it in front of his mouth as Natalie's family watched her watch him eat the entire slice.

"Riveting stuff!" Marcus said, then jammed a slice into his mouth.

The group's attention swung to the idiot podiatrist, and everyone had to be thinking the same thing.

How the hell had this man made it through grade school —let alone podiatry school?

But he owed the guy for drawing the family's quizzical gazes off of him.

"Sorry," he said under his breath as Natalie chose a slice of cheese.

"It's okay. We'll have time tonight to get our stories straight," she whispered back.

Damn right. Everything was riding on them keeping up this con for another reason.

Charlie knew he was at the camp.

The text he'd received in the van had come from his boss, asking for an update, and the words he'd quickly hammered out in response flashed through his mind.

Met a Woolwich granddaughter on the flight. She invited me to stay at the camp with her. Nothing is standing in my way.

Now, he needed to stick to his plan and use this opportunity to get to know Hal and Bev and see what made them tick. Then, he could start the delicate work of convincing them to sell—and offer up his company as the perfect conduit to attaining that deal.

"So, Hal, how's everything going with the business? It's strange you're not running a camp session this summer," Leo asked, shifty-eyed as he tucked into a slice, and Jake's ears perked up.

Maybe it would be easier than he thought to get the dirt on Camp Woolwich.

Hal shared a look with Bev. "We wanted to celebrate the fiftieth anniversary of the camp and our wedding anniversary with the people we love most without the pressure of preparing for the campers."

"But won't the lost revenue be a hit?" the man pressed.

"Our lost revenue is no worry of yours, Leo," Hal answered with an edge, his New England accent growing thicker.

Leslie shared a look with Bev. "We want to make sure you both are well taken care of. Leo and I love Camp Woolwich so much, but if it's become too much to maintain, there are options."

"Your grandfather and I are quite fine, dear," Bev added with a warm grin, the measured yin to Hal's hard yang.

"I think I can speak for all the Woolwich grandchildren when I say that all we want is for you both to enjoy these golden years," Leslie cooed.

Natalie set her plate down hard, and the clang of the dish brought all eyes their way.

"You'd never sell the camp, would you?" Natalie asked.

Bev waved her off. "Kids, we love you, but this is a cele-bration! There will be no talk of business! Your grandfather and I are fine. The camp is fine. Now, we've got you all tucked away in the three honeymoon cabins. I suggest you head over and get a good night's rest. All the festivities start tomorrow after breakfast."

Bev and Hal ushered the cousins and their husbands toward the front door, but Natalie hung back, boxing up the leftover pizza and tidying up the kitchen.

He collected the dishes from the table and set them next to the sink. "Are you all right?"

She stared out the window at the dark water below. "I don't understand why Leslie and Leo would even suggest that my grandparents part with Camp Woolwich. Those two have never shown interest in the camp before."

He schooled his features. His work started now. "Your grandparents are getting older, and fifty years is a long time to run a business."

She played with the edge of a dishtowel. "But they love it. This place is who they are."

This was the kind of bullshit attachment he'd never allow of himself.

She shook her head. "I'm sorry to trouble you with this. I

promised you peace and relaxation, and here you are, smack dab in the middle of Woolwich family business."

He met her gaze in the window's reflection. "I don't mind. And remember, I also agreed to be your fake Jake. If that means family pizza parties and meat-eating demonstrations, I'm good with that."

She turned to him, and her ocean green eyes sparkled with gratitude. "You're a good Jake, you know that?"

He wasn't a good Jake. A good Jake wouldn't be weighing his options on how to get the land she loved at the best price. But she didn't need a good Jake. She just needed a Jake, and that's all he could ever be to her. Still, unlike every other deal he'd closed, he'd never experienced the strange twinge he felt pulling tight in his chest that absolutely, positively could not be guilt. He didn't do guilt, right?

Bev entered the kitchen and frowned. "Go on, you two. You've had a long day, and you'll need your rest. Breakfast will be served bright and early in the dining hall at eight sharp."

Natalie hugged her grandmother. "You'd let me know if you needed anything, right?"

Bev smoothed a lock of her granddaughter's hair behind her ear. "Your grandfather and I are fine, sweetheart."

"Thank you for dinner, Mrs. Woolwich," he added, ignoring that bothersome pang, and reminded himself for a second damn time that he didn't do guilt.

Bev patted his arm. "None of that Mrs. Woolwich business. I'm just Bev around here."

He nodded, holding the woman's emerald gaze that matched her granddaughter's then followed Natalie out the back door and onto a dirt trail, heading away from the water's edge and into the thick coastal foliage.

Natalie walked next to him, silently twisting the sleeve of

her coat as they followed the path. Worry creased her brow as that damn twist in his chest returned. He had to change the subject and get her mind off the camp, but before he could figure out what to say, she pitched forward, snagging her stiletto on a tree root, then clutched onto his arm to stay upright.

"Easy there, Heels," he said, steadying her.

She shook her head and glanced down at her feet. "If I never wear these shoes again, it will be too soon."

He couldn't have her thinking that. He hadn't lied to Leo. Natalie did look damn good in those shoes.

"Let me help," he said.

She took a wobbly step back and raised her hands defensively. "I am not going over your shoulder again, mister."

"How about this?" he said, scooping her up, honeymoon-style.

She wrapped her arms around his neck and kicked her feet playfully. "Is this what you do with all the girls? Seems a little caveman-ish," she added with a giggle that went straight to his cock.

Dammit! He was grateful to get her mind off selling the camp, but his cock had no place in this deal. He could not think about how good she smelled or how sexy she looked in that trench. He especially couldn't think about how much he liked having her in his arms.

"We can't have you falling on your ass," he answered, trying to think of the most practical reason for whisking a woman off her feet, as he continued down the path then veered right toward the rental cottages when she tensed.

"How'd you know which way to go?"

Shit! He wasn't supposed to know anything about Camp Woolwich.

"I figured you'd tell me if I went the wrong way. You must know this place like the back of your hand," he added, steering the conversation away from his slipup.

She relaxed in his arms. "I do. This is my favorite place on earth."

"Oh yeah?" he replied, that damn tightness back in his chest.

She sighed. "The water, the woods. Everything seems so possible here—like it doesn't matter where you've been or what you've done. This place wipes it clean and gives you a fresh start. Whenever I'm here, I see the world with new eyes." She shifted in his arms and held his gaze in the moonlight. "Do you feel it, Jake? It's all around us."

He stilled. "What's all around us?"

She smiled up at him. "Hope."

He inhaled the salty-sweet Maine air as the summer breeze rustled through the trees. The hint of smoke teased his nostrils, and he would have sworn that there was a campfire going nearby, bringing him back to a simpler time, a happier time. Caught between the past and the present, he pictured himself the summer he'd spent here, hiking the trails, exploring the abandoned lighthouse, and jumping off the dock, his arms and legs extended like a starfish and smiling so hard his cheeks hurt. He'd loved the water once. He'd loved the lightness of floating on his back and staring up at the sky.

His gaze slid to Natalie's lips, and the memory of the girl he kissed at the well came rushing back. The kiss that left him feeling invincible. That night, in his cot, after he'd watched from behind a tree as she made it safely inside her cabin, he'd promised himself that he'd find her. Sure, it was the last night of camp, but they could write to each other. He had it all worked out and had even pictured his desk drawers, teeming with delicately addressed stamped envelopes from her, whoever she was.

But he'd never gotten the chance to find her. Not when his uncle, and not his parents, arrived to collect him from camp.

He swallowed back the memories and tightened his grip on Natalie's lithe body. It was as if holding on to her gave him the strength to stay rooted in that moment, safe from the ghosts of his past.

He swallowed past the lump in his throat. "Yes, I feel the hope."

"Then you get it," she replied with a smile so genuine all he wanted to do was kiss her to get a taste of the near-palpable joy that radiated off her.

"You're going to get it if you don't join us for truth or dare," came Lara's high-pitched shriek of a laugh followed by footsteps scurrying over the top of the hill.

What the hell?

Natalie dropped her head to his shoulder. "I figured we'd outgrown that."

"Come on, Jake and Nat! It's a camp tradition," came Leslie's equally grating voice.

He started up the hill as the flickering light of a campfire, and a trio of compact cottages came into view.

He glanced over at Team Podiatry, sitting around a firepit. "How many camp traditions are there around here?"

She groaned. "Too many to count. It may be better if we get it over with. Lara has the attention span of a fruit fly, so hopefully, this won't take long."

"Aren't you the gentleman, carrying Nat all the way to the honeymoon cottages," Lara crooned from her spot next to her husband.

Leslie waved them over. "Sit! We've got the fire going,

and it's a Woolwich tradition to play truth or dare on the first night of camp."

"This really isn't camp, Les," Natalie replied as he gently set her down.

"We're *at* camp, so it *is* camp," Leslie snapped over the flames.

He met the woman's hard gaze. When this deal went through, he would need to add a clause that this bitch didn't get a penny. But when Natalie touched his arm, all the malice drained away as they sat down on a bench across from Leo and Leslie. He was no relationship expert, but even he could feel the waves of tension passing between the two of them. For a married couple, they didn't seem to like each other very much.

"Okay! Okay! Okay! Truth or dare, Nat," Lara clucked, clapping her hands.

Natalie turned to him, wide-eyed, and he understood her unease. They couldn't choose truth because they hadn't worked all that out yet.

"Dare," she answered.

Leo leaned forward as the fire lit his creepy as hell expression. "I dare you to take off your shoes and run around the firepit five times."

This foot freak!

Jake squared his jaw. "Hell, no, Dr. Dix. And this is your last warning about Natalie and the foot shit. The only person here that gets to touch Natalie's feet is me."

He pinned the man with his gaze. He needed Dr. Tootsie Toucher to get the message loud and clear.

"Then kiss her," Leslie barked, cutting through the testosterone haze.

"Right here? In front of everyone?" Natalie asked.

"Kiss! Kiss! Kiss!" Lara and Marcus cheered.

Leslie crossed her arms. "That's the dare."

Natalie gave him a nervous smile. "A quick kiss couldn't hurt."

Quick kiss. Okay, he could do this. He leaned in and pecked her lips.

Bing, bang, boom! Done.

Leslie groaned. "Oh my, God! You guys look about as comfortable kissing as two thirteen-year-olds before they have to give it up for the Kiss Keeper. After five months and six days, you have slept together, right?"

In a flurry of awkward responses, Natalie said yes just as he'd shot back a resounding no.

"So, you have, or you haven't?" Leslie demanded.

Natalie nodded emphatically. "We have. We totally have. Remember that time we had intercourse at that...hotel."

They could not screw this up. That stink-eyed Leslie already seemed to be on to them.

He nodded to his fake girlfriend. "Yeah, and then, there was that time we had intercourse in a...bed," he added and immediately wanted to head-butt himself.

Intercourse? What was this? High school sex ed?

Sweet Christ! They sounded like idiots.

"Twice? That's it?" Leo questioned.

"That was...one day. We like to do it several times a day," Natalie countered with a nonchalant wave of her hand.

He turned to her. "We do?"

She nodded, her eyes begging him to go along. "We do."

He turned to Leslie and Leo and plastered on his best shit-eating grin. "We do."

Leslie's features hardened. "Then let's see a real kiss. It can't be hard for you guys, especially if you're screwing multiple times a day."

Natalie twisted the belt of her trench coat. "Sure, we can—"

But before she finished whatever the hell she was going to say, he cupped her face in his hands and pressed his lips to hers, and the earth shifted off its axis.

He'd kissed a lot of women, but it had been years since a kiss had taken over all his senses.

Natalie's sweet gasps and petal-soft lips had him reeling. He watched as the shock in her eyes disappeared. She blinked them closed and leaned in, pressing her hands to his chest. They fit together like the last piece of a puzzle, clicking into place, no doubt as to where they belonged in the world. He tilted her head, and she sighed, allowing their tongues to meet in a sensual ebb and flow of warm, wet heat.

"Natalie," he whispered, pulling back a fraction before sliding her onto his lap.

He needed to have her closer. He wanted every part of her pressed to him. She threaded her fingers into the hair at the nape of his neck, and his cock strained against his pants. Her breaths came in tight gasps, and he gripped her ass, shifting her body to straddle him as her breasts pressed against his chest, and her soft, supple curves met his hard angles.

He wasn't one for kissing. He was more of a get-to-the-fucking guy. But he'd gladly kiss Natalie Callahan all night long. Unfortunately, a blow to his arm put the brakes on their kissing session.

He stared at the ground where an ugly as hell shoe rested, then glanced over at Leslie, wild-eyed, with another Dr. Scholl's clog in her hand, ready to throw in their direction.

"Time-out, Porn Hub! We said to kiss, not dry-hump!" Leslie bit out then chucked the shoe.

This time, he was ready and caught it then tossed it to the ground. But he didn't give a damn about a pair of orthopedic shoes and turned his attention back to the beautiful trench-wearing brunette on his lap.

"I think we nailed truth or dare. Are you ready to call it a night?"

Natalie brushed her fingertips over her kiss-swollen lips. "Okay," she replied on a dreamy exhale.

"Okay," he echoed, trying to sound all business and not reveal that their first kiss may have been the best kiss of his life as he lifted her back into his arms.

Natalie glanced around the courtyard in a daze. "Which cottage is ours?"

"The one on the far right!" Lara chirped, then held out her phone. "Hey, do you guys want to see the video of that meat-eating show? Marcus found it!"

"Shut up, Lara!" Leslie bit out, then stormed off toward one of the darkened cottages with Leo, plucking his wife's shoes from the ground, then skulking back to their cabin.

Jake shared a look with Natalie. It was like they were in the twilight zone.

He turned to podiatry's Tweedledum and Tweedledee. "Thanks for the offer, Marcus, but we're going to pass on that meat video. Maybe another time."

"Sure thing, dude!" Marcus replied, sounding more like a surfer than a doctor.

Jake shrugged off the crazy-town cousins and followed the dirt path up to the darkened cottage. He shifted a still-dazed Natalie in his arms to open the door then whisked her inside.

"So that kiss..." he remarked as he set her down.

It was better to address it and move on.

She turned on a lamp, and a warm pool of light lit the cozy space. "Probably, a good thing to get out of the way. And, now, we don't have to worry about my cousins wondering if we've had intercourse."

He stared at her lips. Why couldn't he stop staring at her lips?

He blinked, but it didn't help. "Can we stop saying intercourse?"

Natalie cocked her head to the side. "What's wrong with intercourse?"

"Nothing is wrong with intercourse. I love intercourse," he sputtered.

"Then why can't we say it?" she pressed.

That kiss. That amazing as hell kiss had turned his mind to mush.

He took a step toward her. "Because every time you say intercourse, all I want—"

"Is to have intercourse," she finished.

They stood in the dim room, staring at each other.

"We are two people hypothetically capable of intercourse," he mused, taking another step toward her.

"And, even though I'm done with Jakes, you're my fake Jake so, I wouldn't be breaking my no Jake rule," she offered up, then took a step.

"Right, I don't count as a real Jake," he agreed, inching forward.

"And I'm on the pill, so we wouldn't have to worry about any hypothetically unplanned events," she answered, moving closer.

"And I've been tested, and I'm clean," he added, closing the distance between them.

Their bodies only inches apart, she exhaled a shaky breath. "Me, too."

He reached for the belt of the trench coat and twisted the fabric around his fingers. "So, hypothetically, nothing is stopping us."

"Nothing," she answered.

He'd never been so turned on from such a super-nerdy hypothetical intercourse discussion.

A sultry hint of a smile pulled at the corners of Natalie's mouth, and she glanced down at the trench coat belt, twisted around his fingers.

"How are you with knots?"

"I'm the damn knot master," he replied, making quick work of the belt tied around her waist. The coat fell open, and he was met with creamy skin and black lace.

"I love this dress," he said, his tone growing low and primal.

Jake number six was an idiot.

Standing before him in red heels and sexy lingerie was a literal goddess, and as fake Jake number seven, he wasn't about to screw this up.

He traced his index finger along the edge of the lacy bra cup. "What do you say we give this intercourse thing a shot?"

She held his gaze, then slid the coat past her shoulders. The material fell to the ground and pooled around her stilettos.

She took his tie into her hands and skimmed her fingers down the silk. "Oops! I seem to be almost naked. This seems like an excellent time to engage in some intercourse."

That it did. And Jake Teller didn't need to be told twice.

He took her into his arms and kissed her in a fiery crash of lips and tongues and teeth. She kicked off her heels and melted into him, wrapping her arms around his neck as he gripped her ass and lifted her into his arms. She bucked against him, and he pressed her back against the wall, pinning her body tightly to his. The cottage wasn't that large, more of a glorified studio. But between the bed, a table, and old rocking chair, he'd identified plenty of surfaces to screw his fake girlfriend's brains out.

His kisses drifted from her mouth to her jawline as he pumped his hips, and Natalie's breathy gasps and carnal moans flipped a switch in his brain, sharpening his mind on one single objective.

Make this woman come all night long.

She tugged at his jacket. "Why are you still in that suit?"

That was a good question.

He walked them over to the bed and plopped her onto the mattress. With a surprised gasp and a giggle, she leaned back onto her elbows and settled herself on the bed. The dim light cast her in an ethereal glow, and with her tousled dark hair and those mesmerizing green eyes, his gaze devoured her body.

He loosened his tie and tossed it onto the bed. Then, buttons popping, he stripped out of his dress shirt and kicked off his shoes, pants, and boxers.

Slowly, he prowled the length of her body, trailing his lips from her ankles, up her calves, and past her thighs. She gasped as he slid the silky G-string down her legs.

"You're like a work of art," he growled against her thigh, nipping the sensitive skin when a flash of royal blue caught his eye, and he reached for his tie, dragging the soft material between her breasts.

"What are we going to do with this?" she purred, working the material between her fingers.

He thought back to when he helped her with the sleep mask. "Lift your head," he directed.

She complied, and he covered her eyes, fashioning a makeshift blindfold, then positioned his cock between her thighs.

"I'm going to lick and suck every inch of your body."

She bit her lip as he teased her entrance with the tip of his cock.

Without the gift of sight, her hands slid down his back, greedily exploring his body until she reached his ass and dug her nails into his flesh. He sucked in a tight breath, wanting to drive in hard. He tensed, so ready to have her calling out his name in ecstasy when he stared down at her and stilled as a wave of familiarity crashed over him. He liked having her blindfolded. He liked it a lot. He wasn't much into the kink, but this felt right.

"Are you ready?" he whispered against the shell of her ear.

"Yes," she gasped.

Desire thrummed between them as he thrust inside her and was met with her sweet, warm heat.

With her blindfolded, he stared down at her and pumped his hips. He liked watching her. He'd never noticed the little things about the women he'd fucked. But with Natalie, every gasp and every sigh drew him in, deeper and deeper. He slid his hand down the side of her body and cupped her ass, changing the angle to deepen his penetration and grind against her sensitive bundle of nerves.

He dialed up his pace, and she wrapped her arms around him, anchoring her body to his. Lust and need hammered through his veins as he worked her into a frenzy. An ocean, raging with a feverish intensity, threatened to swallow them whole. But he needed more. He needed all of her. Removing the blindfold, he met her gaze and cupped her face in his hand. He kissed her and swallowed her sweet cries of pleasure as she met her release, and he couldn't hold back. Lost somewhere between the past and the present, a storm thundered through him, and he flew over the edge. The coil wound tight in his belly exploded with a rush of heat and euphoria.

He'd been guarded for so long, this freedom to let go, to give himself over so unreservedly felt as if someone had handed him a get out of jail free card. A wave of peaceful bliss he hadn't known in years engulfed him as they came back from ecstasy's abyss.

A tangle of arms and legs, he smoothed a lock of hair behind her ear.

"That was some...intercourse," she said, catching her breath.

He chuckled. That word would never sound the same to him again. He shifted his body off of her and covered them with a worn quilt from the end of the bed.

"Are you like this with all your fake girlfriends?" she asked, resting her head in the crook of his neck, and the tightness returned to his chest.

He wasn't like this with anyone. It had to be this place. It had to be the memories of who he used to be that brought all his defenses crashing down. He didn't have the luxury of being like this with anyone, especially her. Emotional ties made a person vulnerable and weak, and in his world, love and control couldn't coexist.

And more importantly, he wasn't just here to pretend to be Natalie Callahan's boyfriend.

He was here to get her family's land—the only thing standing between himself and complete control of his life.

She hummed a sleepy sigh against his neck. "Good night, Fake Jake."

He stared at the ceiling of the cottage. That's who he was, Fake Jake. He could write off tonight as a lapse in judgment. But from this point on, he'd need to keep his cock in his pants and his eyes on the prize.

6

Ding! Ding! Ding! Ding!

Natalie tried to move but couldn't. It wasn't an unpleasant feeling. In fact, it was quite lovely—like sleeping in a cocoon—when something hard pressed against her ass.

This was no ordinary cocoon.

She blinked open her eyes and glanced down to find a muscled and nicely tanned arm wrapped around her torso. And that something hard pressed to her backside? That was the magical cock of her fake boyfriend.

The first Jake to make her come.

Oh, she'd slept with the other Jakes. She'd twisted herself into a pretzel for each one, trying to be whatever woman she thought they'd wanted. Unfortunately, that meant faking a lot of orgasms.

But there was no faking the rush of carnal release that tore through her last night with her fake Jake. Nope, that round of intercourse didn't require any pretending or sneaking away to finish herself off after an unsatisfying roll in the hay with a lackluster Jake.

It was still hard to believe that twenty-four hours ago,

she'd thought her day was going to include a job offer and then a trip to Maine with her boyfriend.

Instead, she was here with Jake Teller. That's what the TSA agent and the gate agent had called him, right?

OMG! She was only about eighty-six percent sure that was his name.

What a little vixen she'd become! Her mind went back to Jake number four. The jerk who'd said she wasn't adventurous enough in bed. Well, screw you, Jake number four! Wait! She did not want to screw number four again. But look at her now, having mind-blowing sex with Jake number seven.

But he wasn't Jake number seven.

He didn't count as one of her Jakes, and she couldn't get attached to this one. Even with his magical penis, he was still a Jake, and she was done with Jakes.

Done.

And then it hit her. Maybe ditching the Jakes would break the stupid Kiss Keeper Curse! Could the Jakes be to blame? Yes, it was crazy to blame a lifetime of bad luck on her dating pool of Jakes, but she had to do something, change something. And she would—after she got through this week with the help of her final Jake.

She craned her head back to get a look at her spooning partner when his hand slid from where it rested on her belly, and he cupped her breast. His thumb stroked the tight peak of her nipple as her body trembled, clearly remembering all the delicious things this man had done to it last night.

"Jake?" she whispered.

"Hmm," he hummed as his hips rocked against her lazily.

Was he even awake? Was he this good of a lover even when he was unconscious?

"You smell so good," he mumbled sleepily against the shell of her ear, and a shiver danced its way down her spine.

This man's gravelly morning voice could melt panties.

Lucky for her, she wasn't wearing any.

Half-awake, a fully erect fake Jake slid his cock past her delicate folds. Warmth pooled between her thighs as they made love slowly in a tangle of lazy limbs. She released a low hum of satisfaction when the distant sound of a bell carried in on the morning breeze.

Ding! Ding! Ding!

They froze.

"Is this real?" he asked, the grogginess replaced with a perplexed bend to his words.

She needed a little clarification. "What exactly are you asking about? There's a decent amount of fake and real stuff going on between us."

"This. Me, taking you from behind," he replied.

She turned and caught his gaze out of the corner of her eye. "That part is real."

He released her body, scrambled away, then sprang out of bed. "Jesus, I thought I was dreaming!" he said, running his hands down his face.

She wrapped the quilt around her body and stared at him, wide-eyed. He glanced around the cottage and pulled a doily off an end table and held it in front of his still very erect cock.

She couldn't look away. "You need a bigger doily."

"What?" he asked, completely confused.

She waved her hand toward his crotch. "I can still see your..."

"Shit!" he whisper-shouted, dropping the doily and substituting it with a carved wooden mallard.

This was weird. They'd slept together last night, and he'd seemed ready for round two until...

Ding! Ding!

She dragged her eyes from the mallard penis protector and met his gaze. "That was two dings!"

At Camp Woolwich, you lived by the bells. And two rings meant five minutes until breakfast.

And you did not want to be late for breakfast.

"We need to go!" she cried, throwing off the quilt and sprinting to her suitcase.

"Five minutes, right?" he called from the other side of the room.

"Yeah, and if my grandparents are running this anniversary week like a camp, which I'm pretty sure they are, we do not want to be late."

She yanked a bra and a pair of panties out of her suitcase, Houdinied herself into the garments at Mach speed, then shimmied into a T-shirt dress and pulled on a pair of sneakers. She glanced over at Jake and caught an eyeful of her fake boyfriend's ripped back as he threw on a T-shirt and cargo shorts then pulled on a ball cap.

He turned to her, and she smoothed her dress.

"Do I look okay?"

His gaze softened for a fraction of a second before he schooled his features. "Yeah, you look fine."

"I think we can still make it on time. Let's go," she said, pivoting toward the door when she stepped on one of her sneaker's laces and pitched forward, falling ass over elbow, and twisted her ankle. She touched the tender flesh, then glanced up at her fake boyfriend. "I think I tweaked it."

"Shit!" he whispered and scooped her up.

This caveman carrying routine was starting to feel remarkably normal.

"I can probably walk," she said, bouncing as he sprinted out of the cottage and down the path toward the camp dining hall.

"No time!" he bit out, dodging rocks and muddy spots as the final bell rang.

One minute.

Jake huffed-it down the path as Fish was coming up.

"You're the last two to breakfast," he called with a wink.

Shoot! Shoot! Shoot!

Jake rounded the corner then slung open the dining hall's old screen door. The hinges whined their protest as Jake thundered into the room like a wide receiver, leaping in the air to make a touchdown before the clock ran out, and all eyes landed on them.

"Good morning," her grandfather said, raising an eyebrow.

He stood next to her grandmother at the front of the room as table upon table of Woolwiches and Woolwich family friends cocked their heads to check out the late arrivals.

"Did we make it?" Jake huffed on a winded breath.

"Barely," her grandfather answered.

She scanned the room with an apologetic smile, but nobody looked all that surprised. And, of course, they didn't. She was the screw-up Woolwich granddaughter.

But wait! She wasn't—at least, not entirely.

She glanced up at her breathless fake boyfriend and plastered on a wide grin. "Hey, everyone! This is Jake."

"Hi, Jake," replied the room in unison.

"Does he ever let you walk?" Leslie asked from a table near the front of the room.

"I tweaked my ankle, but I'm sure it's nothing."

"I could take a look," Leo said, coming to his feet, but, as quickly as he popped up, he sat down and proceeded to study his oatmeal.

She glanced over to find her fake boyfriend, stone-faced, pinning the podiatrist with his gaze, and a grateful warmth flooded her chest. Jake was three for three on thwarting Leo's attempts to go all foot freak on her.

She turned her attention to her grandparents. "Sorry we're late, we were—"

"Having sex," Lara supplied with the enthusiasm of a game show hostess. "I can only imagine that doing it multiple times a day really eats into your schedule."

Leslie elbowed her sister. "Hush, Lara! What the hell is wrong with you?"

Nat glanced around the room. Thank God, the kids' table was situated all the way back in the far corner of the dining hall. Despite a few little heads popping up to try to get a look over the sea of adults, she knew, from her many years being seated at that very table, that they probably didn't hear Lara's sex observation.

She recycled her apologetic grin. "No, we were about to leave when I tripped. That's why we're late."

"We figured since we heard you guys at it, last night, maybe you were knocking another one out this morning," Marcus chimed brightly as if he were remarking on the weather.

Nat stared at Lara and her husband. She should be embarrassed, but all she could do was wonder how the hell did these people treat actual medical conditions.

"Go on, you two, and take a seat. There are a few spots left at the kids' table," her grandmother said with an amused twinkle in her eye.

"Kids' table?" Jake murmured under his breath.

"Believe me. It beats sitting with my cousins," she whispered back. "Oh, and you can put me down now."

Gently, he eased her out of his arms, and she took a few steps with every eyeball, except for Leo's, trained on her feet.

"All good with the ankle," she said, taking Jake's hand and leading him through the maze of tables to the one littered with half-eaten bowls of oatmeal and torn open mini boxes of cereal.

The hum of table conversations resumed as she and Jake settled into their seats.

"Aunt Nat! Aunt Nat!" the kids cried, abandoning their chairs to cluster around her.

"Wow, you guys have gotten big," she said, staring at six smiling faces. "Jake, meet Annabelle, age six, Finn who's twelve, Maddie and Josie, our nine-year-olds, and the twins, Toby and Tucker, who just turned seven. Did I get that right?"

"Yep, but I'm four minutes older than Tuck," Toby replied with a toothy grin.

Jake glanced around wide-eyed as if rebel forces were invading. "Are these all your nieces and nephews?"

She shook her head. "Technically, I'm not their aunt. I don't have any siblings, so I don't have any official nieces or nephews. These are some of my cousins' kids. But it's easier for them to call me Aunt Natalie instead of first cousin once removed, Natalie," she answered as a tiny body wiggled its way onto her lap.

"This is the table for the six-to twelve-year-olds, Uncle Jake," her lap inhabitant, Annabelle Woolwich, announced proudly with a milk mustache.

"Here, Uncle Jake! You can have a box of Frosted Flakes. Mimi and Poppy said we can have sugar cereal this week!"

Tucker exclaimed, shaking the box a few inches from Jake's face, but the man didn't move.

"Thanks, Tuck," she said, intercepting the cereal box meant for a glazed-over Jake.

"All right, guys! Why don't you finish your breakfast while I talk with Jake for a second?"

The children scrambled back to their seats, and she turned to her overwhelmed date.

"Are you breathing?"

The man had gone rigid and sat there, blinking like a deer caught in a pair of headlights. A pretty standard response after one's first encounter with the entire Woolwich clan. Plus, their chaotic, mad dash start to the day hadn't helped either.

"My family can be...a lot," she offered

"Yeah."

"Here's Woolwich 101. Mimi and Poppy are what the great-grandkids call my grandparents."

Jake nodded as Annabelle opened his box of cereal and poured it into a bowl along with a splash of milk. She handed him a spoon, and he accepted it robotically.

"My grandparents are big on stages and phases. The six-to-twelve table is a big step up from dining with your parents to sitting with the kids for meals. The thirteen-to-fifteen-year-olds are allowed to sit wherever they want and roam around camp on their own."

"What about the older kids?" Jake asked through a bite of cereal.

She gestured with her chin a few tables over to where a group of older teens with bedhead and their gazes all pointed toward their laps sat silently.

"They're probably doing Snapchat or snap cat. Whatever it is, they're glued to their phones. I asked my grandpa if he minded that they barely made a peep or socialized with anyone."

Jake spooned up another bite. "What did he say?"

She grinned. "He asked if I could remember saying anything worth hearing when I was that age. I couldn't."

Jake chuckled. "Makes sense. Those are some crazy years."

"Yeah, I was pretty awkward during that time in my life," she offered.

"I was pretty angry," he replied into his bowl of half-eaten cereal.

Angry?

From his cool demeanor and take-charge attitude, she'd pictured him as someone who'd always had it together. She chose a bowl of oatmeal off a large tray in the center of the table and took a bite, glancing over at her fake boyfriend.

Was there more to him? That was a stupid question. There had to be. Everyone had a past. This Jake just seemed so sure of who he was. She was twenty-eight and flailing from job to job and Jake to Jake. He seemed so solid. She closed her eyes, remembering the tenderness in his gaze before they made love and the strange recognition that passed between them as he worked her body into a frenzy. It was like kissing someone from a past life.

And the sex.

A delicious tingle danced through her body. On a scale of one to ten, she was a solid two when it came to the intimacy department. She'd spent so much energy trying to figure out what her Jake du jour wanted that she'd never focused on herself. But last night, in her fake boyfriend's arms, she couldn't tell where he began and where she ended. And his lips. Just the thought of kissing him had her clenching her core muscles.

And that brought her to his cock. His perfect, thick, hard...

"Natalie?" came a deep voice.

She startled from her daydream and gasped. "I wasn't thinking about cock." She glanced around to find her grandfather frowning and every person, including the owner of the cock she'd been fantasizing about, staring at her.

"Tails," she threw out immediately. "Cocktails," she added, then grabbed a kid-sized cup of apple juice and knocked it back, hoping she hadn't turned completely beet-red from mortification.

"It's eight thirty in the morning, Nat," her grandfather replied, his frown still in place while her grandmother stood silently, lips pressed together, holding back a grin.

"But it's got to be five o'clock somewhere," she parried back, trying to be funny.

Jesus! When would she learn? She wasn't funny!

But an amused little snort from Jake made her feel like less of an idiot. Maybe she was funny, or maybe he was laughing at her? Oh, God! What did it matter?

She glanced over at him, and he tossed her a wink.

The warmth that had flooded her chest earlier was back. Funny. He thought she was funny.

"Natalie, are you all right?" her grandmother asked from the front of the room.

"I'm fine. Maybe a bit jet lagged."

Her grandfather barked out a cough, then crossed his arms. "What is your answer? Yes or no?"

She watched the man closely, and a pang of worry set in. His bright eyes weren't as intense, and he'd lost a bit of weight since she'd last seen him.

Jake leaned in. "While you were meditating back there, they asked if we'd lead the kids' activities this week."

"Of course, I...we'd," she glanced at Jake. "We'd be happy to."

The children at the table clapped and cheered their approval when she felt Jake back at her ear.

"What does that mean?"

She nudged him with her shoulder. "It means that we aren't doing dishes or cleaning the latrine. Everyone gets assigned a job at camp."

"Good call on the kids' stuff," he replied with a grimace as her grandpa began addressing the group.

"Bev and I would like to thank everyone for joining us for our fiftieth anniversary. We've got a schedule full of activities planned with everything culminating on Woolwich Island for our vow renewals," her grandpa said, then turned to her grandmother. "You've put up with me for forty-nine more years than I deserved."

"Try forty-nine and a half," her grandmother replied with a sly grin.

Her grandparents shared a look—the same look she'd loved since she was a little girl. With just a glance, she'd never seen two people more in tune with one another. She'd made a game of it as a girl, observing them closely and counting each gentle nod and every sweet twist of her grandfather's lips when he caught her grandmother's eye. She'd collected these tender moments over the years, tucking them safely away, all the time hoping that, one day, she'd find a special person who looked at her the way her grandfather looked at her grandmother. But with that damn curse and a string of terrible Jakes, what were the chances?

"Here, you can use this," Jake said, breaking into her thoughts and handing her a napkin.

"Why do you think I need that?" she asked.

His gaze softened. "Because you're crying."

She brushed her fingertips across her cheeks, then took the offered napkin and blotted beneath her eyes. "Sorry, my grandparents are so..."

He cupped her face in his hand and wiped a tear away with his thumb. "Yeah, I can tell," he whispered with a faraway look in his eyes. The moment hung there, sweet and tender, but as quickly as it began, it ended when Jake pulled his hand away as if he'd touched a hot stove.

What was going on between them?

That was a stupid question because she knew the answer. Nothing. This was all a big con. Too bad her heart, her silly heart, begged to differ. But with this Jake, she'd have to rely on her head if she wanted to protect her heart. With her resolve intact, she steadied herself and focused on her grandpa's speech.

"We're here to celebrate family and friendship. Everyone in this room has a connection to Camp Woolwich. But even without the cabins or the lodge or the boats and the waterfront, our connection to each other will always live on. Our memories and the stories we tell are as constant as the ocean and just as everlasting."

The breath caught in her throat. Again, another strange veiled reference to change. She stared at her grandparents as they continued to welcome guests and muse about their fifty years together, raising a family and running Camp Woolwich—something that Jake must find horribly dull. But when she'd glanced over at him, he seemed riveted, soaking in every word.

Was he that good at pretending?

She balled up the napkin and sighed. She'd try to find a quiet moment to speak with her grandparents, away from her cousins, to get some answers. But until then, she could pretend she had it all together—at least, partially together—

with Jake. Her last Jake. No, he wasn't hers, but boy, did she feel like she was his last night and this morning with his—

"Aunt Nat! Are you ready?" the twins Toby and Tucker asked in unison.

She startled. The dining hall was near empty. "Am I what?"

"You were doing that thing again," Jake said, biting back a grin.

"What thing?"

His cheeks grew pink. "Zoning out. At least this time, you didn't scream—"

"Okay," she said with a clap of her hands, cutting off her fake boyfriend. "Who's ready for a little outdoor art?"

"Outdoor art? You can't do art outside. At school, we do art at a table," Finn remarked.

She waved the children in. "I've got a secret to tell you. You can do art anywhere."

"Anywhere?" Annabelle asked, wide-eyed.

Nat tapped the little girl's nose. "Anywhere."

"On the moon?" Finn pressed with a sour expression, but she wasn't surprised to find the boy acting cross. The oldest children at the kids' table always felt like they were stuck with a bunch of babies.

She scratched her head, pretending to be stumped, then gasped. "I've got it! You could sprinkle moon dust on drawing paper or make rubbings of astronaut footprints."

The boy pursed his lips. "Yeah, I guess that would work."

"Aunt Nat, can we take the canoes or even sail over to the island?" Josie asked.

"The island? Is that what your grandfather was talking about?" Jake asked, his complexion turning from a healthy tan to a sickly dishwater gray.

She watched him closely. "Yes, Woolwich Island. It's

across from the cove. It's a small island my family uses and sometimes rents out for weddings and events. It's only accessible by water." She pointed out the window that looked out onto the waterfront. "You can see it right there. It doesn't take long to get to."

Jake swallowed hard, the muscles of his throat constricting.

Something about the island had set him off, and she couldn't risk the guy picking up and bolting. To be fake-dumped at a family gathering would be worse than if she'd shown up with no boyfriend at all.

She turned to the children. "How about we explore the trails around camp?"

"Can we take the one with all the good climbing trees?" Tucker asked.

"Sure," she answered, keeping a considerably less pale Jake in the corner of her eye. "Now, you've got two minutes to find the art basket. If I remember right, Mimi keeps it in the lodge next to the art room. Your job is to find it and then meet Jake and me at the flagpole." She glanced at her watch. "Ready, set, go!" she called, and the children ran out of the dining hall in a tangle of whoops and elbows.

The screen door banged shut, and she touched Jake's arm. "Are you okay?"

He shot a glance toward the cove. "I don't do water."

"Do you not know how to swim?"

"I can swim. I just..." he trailed off.

"That's okay. We all have our things. I don't do Jakes anymore," she supplied, trying again to be funny, then immediately felt her cheeks heat.

He cocked his head to the side, and the hint of a smile pulled at the corners of his mouth as the color returned to his chiseled face.

She cringed. "I mean, I'm not going to *date* Jakes, and I guess that also means I shouldn't be doing them either." She stopped talking and covered her face with her hands. "I must sound like an idiot."

"The last thing I'd call you, Natalie, is an idiot," Jake replied as two warm hands rested on top of hers, then gently proceeded to uncover her face.

He threaded their fingers together, and she held his gaze as her pulse kicked up. All it took was one touch from this man, and her heart edged out her head by a landslide.

What was this pull between them? This crazy connection that made her body buzz with anticipation.

He stared down at her, looking as confused as she felt. "It's hard to believe that this time yesterday, we hadn't even met."

"We're on camp time. An hour here is like a day in the real world. At least, that's how it always felt for me. This place is like stepping into an alternate universe where time stands still and, at the same time, seems to go by at the speed of light. You experience life more intensely here. When I was a girl, I'd imagine that I was living inside a work of art—some painting of a far-off, magical place."

"Like being under a spell?" he questioned, leaning in as she pressed up onto her tiptoes.

She nodded as every cell in her body begged to get closer to Jake.

He released her hands and cupped her face. "Your eyes are the exact color of the deepest parts of the water. I always remembered that color. The canopy of green that shimmered in the distance. The vividness. The depth."

No Jake—no, anybody—had ever said anything like that to her before. Was he pretending, simply playing the part of a caring boyfriend? It made no sense to do it now. No one was here. It was only the two of them. Alone.

He slid one hand from her face and trailed his fingertips down her neck, leaving a path of goose bumps as his hand came to rest on her shoulder. His thumb brushed past her collarbone, and a dreamy familiarity washed over her.

"I shouldn't want to kiss you this much," he said on a tight exhale.

"I shouldn't want you to kiss me," she whispered back.

His gaze darkened, and she gripped the fabric of his shirt as his lips hovered a breath away from hers when a chorus of giggles burst their almost-kiss bubble.

She gasped and pulled back to see a frowning Finn flanked by Tucker and Toby, both covering their eyes, as the trio of little girls giggled and squeaked with excitement.

"Do you have the art basket?" she asked, doing her best to recover from that intense almost-kiss.

Finn held up the old wicker case with a corner of drawing paper hanging out of the opening.

"Then we should go," she answered, sharing a quick look with Jake as the children headed for the trail leading away from camp and into the thick foliage.

He held the door for her, and they walked in silence, several paces behind the children.

"I'm sorry. I shouldn't have tried to kiss you," he said with his hands in his pockets.

She stared ahead, needing to collect herself and to remember that he wasn't her Jake. She raised her chin. "It's okay. Like I said, things feel more powerful here. It's part of the—"

"Magic," he supplied.

She nodded as they followed the dirt path into the heart of the woods, then glanced up at him. The softness in his expression had reverted to the stone-faced man she'd met at the airport.

"What do you do when you're not pretending to be somebody's boyfriend?" she asked, hoping to ease the tension.

"I'm in commercial real estate."

"You build things?" she asked.

"Yes," he answered, his voice void of emotion and his gaze trained on the path.

This Jake didn't seem keen on sharing.

"Are you from Colorado?" she pressed, grasping for something benign for them to talk about.

"No."

"Then, where?" she chimed.

A muscle ticked in his jaw. "Michigan."

"Is your family still there?"

"No."

"Well, where are they now?" she tried.

This was going nowhere fast. Maybe he *was* a serial killer. They walked a few more paces when he broke the silence.

"How big is the camp?"

"Like acreage?" she asked, grateful for some shred of conversation.

"Yeah."

"It's pretty big. The camp stretches from the cove up the coast where it meets the Atlantic. I think my grandparents own almost five hundred acres, and then there's a nature preserve that surrounds it, so it feels like there are woods and trees and wildlife for miles."

"Hmm," he answered as if he were ticking off a box.

"My grandfather won the land in a card game," she added—a fact that usually intrigued people.

Jake glanced over at her. "Really?"

"It was a long time ago in Boston. He won the land from some guy, and then he and my grandma got married here the very next day."

Jake glanced around. "They married here?"

"Yeah, right by the water."

"Do you know what this place is worth?" he asked.

No one had ever asked her that question before.

She frowned. "I have no idea. Why would that matter?"

"How much further, Aunt Nat?" Annabelle called, her little body hunched forward and arms dangling as if they'd set off to summit Everest and not walk up the hill into the woods.

"This is far enough. You can tell the kids to stop." Her gaze shifted from Jake to the little girl, but she couldn't get his words out of her mind.

Do you know what this place is worth?

Jake's question dropped like a lead weight, but there had to be a reason why he'd ask.

He was in real estate. Could it simply be professional interest or force of habit? In her case, she could barely go anywhere without something calling to her to be sketched or painted.

She pushed the question aside as they caught up with the children, waving them in to gather around the basket. Opening it, she pulled out a worn box of crayons.

"Pick your favorite color and peel off the paper," she directed.

"The crayon will be naked!" Annabelle exclaimed as Toby and Tucker snickered.

She patted the girl's shoulder. "The crayon doesn't mind because it's an artist tool."

"Artists don't use crayons," Finn huffed.

"They sure do, just watch," she countered.

She peeled the paper off a stubby maroon crayon, then selected a piece of paper. "Art and nature go hand in hand. Think of Picasso's sunflowers or Monet's water lilies," she added, then found a fallen leaf on the ground and, gently placing the paper over it, proceeded to make a rubbing. After only a few strokes, the veins of a pear-shaped birch leaf emerged.

"It's like magic!" Annabelle exclaimed, then ripped the paper off her red crayon.

Finn crossed his arms. "It's a leaf."

She crossed her arms, mimicking the preteen. "I bet you can't do it."

The boy's eyes went wide. "I betcha I can."

She tossed him a crayon, and he snagged a piece of paper, looking hellbent on proving her wrong. And it was just the reaction she wanted.

"You're good with kids," Jake offered.

She watched as Finn centered the paper over a knot on a birch tree trunk and went to work. "Kids are easy. They want to learn and explore even when they act like they don't."

He took a step toward her. "I don't know if I agree that kids are easy, but you sure make it look that way."

She continued to watch as Finn plucked a pinecone for Josie. "My way with kids seems to be the one thing the curse hasn't touched."

"Curse?" he questioned.

She cringed. "It may sound a little silly. It's an old Camp Woolwich legend."

She'd never mentioned the Kiss Keeper's curse to any of her other Jakes, but she'd never brought any of her past Jakes here.

She glanced over at the kids and caught Finn's eye. "I'm

going to show Jake around. We'll only be a minute. Can you keep an eye on your cousins?"

"Sure, Aunt Nat," the boy answered, falling nicely into the role of the teacher's, or in this case, aunt's helper.

She gestured for Jake to follow her and led him up the trail toward...

The well.

It had been years since she'd seen it, but it remained as it had in her memory, a simple circular structure made of stone with a weathered wooden roof. It seemed crazy that something so innocuous could have impacted her life so profoundly. But then again, it wasn't just the well. It was the legend, built on kiss after kiss after kiss, year after year after year.

Jake came to her side then froze. "The well."

She nodded. "It may not look like much, but here at Camp Woolwich, there's an old camp legend that a Kiss Keeper haunts it and demands kisses be offered up here at the well."

She looked at Jake, expecting him to laugh or tell her she was insane to believe in childhood campfire stories. But he didn't do or say anything. He just stared at the well.

She continued. "The way it works is a boy and a girl are chosen to sneak out of their cabins late after lights out to go meet their kiss keeper. But you see, you go blindfolded, so you never see who your kiss keeper is. You're supposed to kiss, here, at the old well. If you don't, legend says you'll be cursed."

"How'd you get cursed?" Jake asked, still staring at the gray stones.

"I met my kiss keeper at the well, but before he could kiss me, night patrol stopped us."

"They caught you?" he whispered.

She shook her head. "No, we hid from them, and then my kiss keeper took off his blindfold and guided me back to my cabin."

"You never kissed?" he asked, his voice barely a rasp.

She couldn't stop herself from smiling. "No, he kissed me but not at the well. He kissed me outside of my cabin." She walked up to the well and ran her fingertips over the smooth stone then glanced over her shoulder at her fake boyfriend. "Do you want to know if I ever figured out the identity of my kiss keeper?"

Nothing moved. No breeze. Not a peep from the kids. It was as if nature itself sat stupefied along with him.

Natalie looked down the path that he knew led to the teen girls' cabin, then brushed her fingers across her lips. A quick, unintentional movement, or perhaps it was muscle memory. But her pink cheeks and the girlish curve to her lips all but confirmed that she'd thought about that kiss just as much as he had.

Not that kiss.

Their kiss.

Sweet Christ! Natalie Callahan was his kiss keeper. Of all the women in all the trench coats in all the airport screening lines, what were the odds of not only meeting her but going along with her con that was really his con to get her family's land?

Ping! Ping! Ping!

The smile faded from her face. "Do you need to get that?"

He frowned. "Get what?"

"Your phone."

Dammit!

He pulled it out to find a text from Charlie, then shoved the phone back into his pocket. "It's not important."

"Well, do you want to know if I ever found my kiss keeper?" she asked again.

He swallowed hard. She never saw him. He'd made sure of it because of all those damn kiss keeper rules. No looking at each other. No disclosing your name. But she was right. They hadn't kissed at the well. He'd never contemplated that their kiss at the cabin didn't count.

"Jake, are you okay?"

He shook his head to get his mind back on track. "I'm fine."

A lie.

He was the furthest thing from fine. No more than three feet away stood the girl, now the woman, who he'd thought about night after night. He'd held onto the memory of her through his darkest days.

He cleared his throat, half dreading and half wanting for her to say that she knew it was him.

He shifted his weight. "Did you ever figure it out?"

She sat down on the edge of the well and glanced inside. "No, I didn't. The funny thing is, I didn't want to kiss a boy back then. No, that's not true. I'd thought about it, but—"

"Was it a good kiss?" he asked, hating himself for asking, but he'd always wondered if it meant as much to her as it had to him.

Her cheeks went all rosy again, and she smiled the same smile he remembered from that night when he left her, standing in the moonlight outside the cabin with her face partially covered by a bandana.

She pressed her fingertips to her lips again. "It was the perfect first kiss."

She wasn't wrong. It was. He remembered everything about that night and everything about her.

His phone pinged again, and he stiffened.

"Is it your work or your family? Are you sure it's not important?" she asked from her perch on the well.

He took out his phone to see another notification of a text from Charlie, then set the device to mute. "I can get to it later."

He had to get his head in the game. But this, finding her, threw one hell of a curveball into his plan. She watched him carefully with those trusting ocean-green eyes. But he wasn't one to be trusted. Even if he wasn't there to persuade her grandparents to sell, he wasn't the man for her.

He wasn't the man for anyone.

He could only imagine that the other Jakes she'd dated were much like the douche canoe he'd watched dump her and move on in real-time. But he was no better. In fact, he may be worse. Maybe once upon a time, there was a chance for him to be one of the good guys—a family man and a loving husband like his father had been—but all that promise and potential evaporated the moment he learned of his parents' deaths.

No, if he wanted the control and the power that he'd focused on achieving for more than half his life, there was only one way forward.

Play the part of Natalie's boyfriend.

Get the grandparents to sell.

Then, move on. He had to treat Camp Woolwich like any other property—like any other deal.

This was business.

"I still wonder about him," she said, breaking into his thoughts.

"About who?" he asked.

She toyed with the hem of her dress. "The boy, my kiss keeper. Where is he now? What's he doing? Does he remember me?"

He joined her at the well, his pulse quickening as if his body remembered what it was like being there with her all those years ago, and then, he was thirteen again. All nerves and lanky limbs, he wanted now what he wanted then. He sat down next to her and drew his fingertips up the smooth, milky-white skin of her neck and cupped her face in his hands.

"I think you'd be a hard person to forget, Heels."

It was the truth. He'd never forgotten her.

She gazed up at him with those damn elusive eyes that made him forget all the darkness and only see her and her light. She was like a beacon drawing him in. He brushed his thumb across her bottom lip, and that force was back, that magnetic pull between them. That intense drive to kiss her, to protect her, and to make love to her flooded his system. He could give in a little bit. Being a good fake boyfriend was all part of the con, right?

"Oh, Jake," she whispered as she closed her eyes.

He threaded his fingers into her hair, and she sighed, melting into his touch. He'd allow himself one last kiss. He leaned in, and the heat of her breath teased his lips, but before they could meet, a loud cry came from where they'd left the children.

"Aunt Nat! Uncle Jake! Come quick!"

He and Natalie broke apart, and she sprang to her feet.

"What is it?" she called as they ran the short distance to where the kids had been making their rubbings.

"It's Toby," Maddie said, pointing up into a giant oak. "He climbed up way too high. We told him to stop."

Finn paced back and forth. "I tried to climb up and help him down, but—"

"I have to pee!" Toby called from way too damn high up a tree, his voice a mix of fear and urgency.

"He says that if he moves, he'll pee his pants," Finn added, shaking his head like a frustrated parent.

"Okay," Natalie said with her hands on her hips, gazing up at Toby's dangling legs. "I've climbed this tree a million times. This is nothing to worry about. I'll go up and get him."

"What if he pees on you?" Annabelle whispered with wide eyes.

Josie wrinkled her nose. "Ew!"

"He won't," Natalie answered.

Tucker glanced up at his brother. "What if he pees on us when you're bringing him down?"

Natalie chewed her lip. "Okay, I've got a solution for that. Everyone, hold hands, and take three giant steps away from the tree."

They quickly complied.

"I've really gotta go!" Toby wailed.

"My mom will be *really* mad if Toby pees his pants, Aunt Nat," Tucker called from the safe zone.

"Yeah, she'll be *really* mad at me," Natalie said under her breath.

"Let me go."

She turned to him. "Jake, you did not sign up for rescuing a seven-year-old with a full bladder from a tree."

He chuckled. "That may be the first time that phrase has ever been uttered."

She dropped her head and sighed. "How good of a climber are you?"

He cracked his knuckles. "Master level."

She raised an eyebrow. "I pretty much lived in this tree when I was a girl."

He schooled his features. "Is that a challenge?"

"Aunt Nat! I can't hold it much longer!"

A playful glint in her eye answered his question.

"Ready, set..." he began.

"Go!" she cried, striding toward the tree.

And sweet baby Jesus! She wasn't kidding. He'd been free climbing for years, but Natalie hit each branch like she was part primate. Except, there was nothing primate about her smooth, toned legs, moving from branch to branch. And then he got a quick glimpse of hot pink lace and the curve of her ass.

"Holy hell," he said, unable to hold back.

Natalie stopped climbing, glanced down at the kids below, and then up at the child, clutching the trunk for dear life before awkwardly pressing her knees together. "Don't you dare look up my dress, Jake Teller!"

He shrugged. "You're the one who cheated to get ahead."

"Aunt Nat, I'm gonna blow!"

"How are we going to do this?" Natalie asked, biting back a grin.

He had to admit that this was pretty damn hilarious.

He pulled his gaze from her ass and looked past her at the dangling shoestrings, several branches up. "You get to him first, since you're part chimpanzee, and then I can carry him down on my back."

"Okay, let's hope this works—commence Operation No Tree Pee," she said, then worked her way up, limb by limb.

It didn't take them long to get to the boy.

"Are you ready, Toby? I'm going to carry you down," he said.

"What if I pee?" the child squealed, clenching every muscle in his little body.

Good question. The last thing he wanted was to be covered in piss.

"See that bush," he said, pointing toward the ground. "Once we get down, we'll race over, and you can pee there."

"Okay," the boy replied, scrunching up his face.

Natalie climbed onto Toby's branch and took his hand. "You can make it, honey. I know you can."

"Are you going to go fast, Uncle Jake?"

"Like a tree ninja, dude," he replied, not sure what a tree ninja was, but it sounded a hell of a lot cooler than a potty porter.

The boy cracked a smile then grimaced. "If I laugh, I'll pee."

"No funny business," Natalie ordered, clearly holding back a grin.

He bit back a smile of his own. "Got it. Commencing Operation No Tree Pee."

Natalie's eyes sparkled as she shook her head, swallowing back a laugh. "All right, Toby, I'm going to help you get down to Jake."

The boy released the tree trunk and, with Natalie's help, lowered himself down.

"Climb onto my back," he said, helping the boy get into place.

He started the decent as the children below began chanting.

"Hold it! Hold it! Hold it!"

"I can't hold it!" Toby yelled.

Jake quickened his pace. "You've got to hold it, Toby!"

"I'm trying, but it's like a giant lake is inside of me."

Jake glanced down. They were so close. "Ten seconds, Toby. You've got this."

He climbed down the tree, navigating the branches and trying like hell not to bounce too much.

"I can't hold it," the boy wailed.

"Five seconds," he called, nearly at the bottom. "Count it down, Toby!"

"Five," the boy yelled along with the other children.

He cleared the last branch and carefully lowered himself and the child to the ground.

"Four!"

He swung Toby around and held the kid out in front of him like a brick of dynamite, ready to blow.

"Three!"

"The bush, Jake! Get him to the bush!" Natalie called.

"Two."

Kicking up bits of dirt and pine needles, he sprinted to the cluster of wild blackberry bushes and set the boy down.

"All you, Toby," he called over his shoulder, scrambling away to avoid a direct hit.

"I can't get my shorts undone," the kid whined.

Jesus Christ on a Cracker!

He spun around and went back. Operation No Tree Pee could not fail. As quickly as possible, he assessed the situation.

"Toby, it looks like the standard button zipper combo."

The boy looked at him with desperation in his eyes. "But, my underwear is stuck in the zipper."

Dammit!

"I'm going to talk you through it. Undo the button, and then you're going to pull the zipper as hard as you can."

Toby had gone beet-red from clenching. "Okay, here goes."

With a growl, Toby yanked the zipper, and his shorts fell past his knobby knees to his ankles. Without a second to lose—because he didn't want to get squirted with pee—Jake leaped over the bush, limbs waving wildly as he made a mad dash back to the group.

Natalie pressed her hand to her heart. "Were you hit?"

He caught his breath and dusted a few errant pine needles from his clothing. "No, I'm good. I made it out just in time," he answered before realizing that she was messing with him.

"See, you're good with kids," she replied with that glint in her eyes.

He pulled a bit of tree bark from her hair. "Just the ones bursting with urine."

"Pretty good teamwork back there, don't you think?" she asked as his hand lingered in her hair.

He stared into her eyes. His kiss keeper's eyes. He'd always wondered what color they were. But his imagination couldn't hold a candle to what it was like to gaze into the real deal.

"Please, tell us you're not going to kiss her, Uncle Jake!" Tucker said.

He and Natalie glanced at the kids and found all but one child covering their eyes.

"We're absolutely not going to kiss," Natalie answered, but she didn't pull away.

"You look like you're going to kiss," cooed Annabelle, who happened to be the only child who didn't look totally freaked out.

"Kissing must be so gross, right, Uncle Jake?" Finn added with his hands covering his eyes.

He shared a look with Natalie. "I wouldn't say it's *so* gross."

Maddie peeked through her fingers. "Aunt Nat, do you like kissing Uncle Jake?"

"Um, sure, I like it," she answered, catching his eye with a what-the-hell-are-we-supposed-to-say expression.

He cleared his throat. "Yeah, it's…"

The best thing ever. Like no sensation he'd ever experienced. Scratch that. It's exactly the best thing he'd ever experienced because she was his kiss keeper. Those lips. That smile. Despite everything that he had on the line, all he wanted to do was take her into his arms, press his lips to hers, and kiss her until the world disappeared.

"It's what?" Natalie asked with a tantalizing curve to her lips.

He stared into her eyes, completely lost. "There's nothing better than kissing your aunt Natalie."

Natalie's gaze softened, drawing him into a place where only love and kindness existed, as the children threw out a chorus of moans and groans but went silent when the camp bell rang.

Ding! Ding! Ding! Ding! Ding!

Five rings!

"It's an emergency!" Annabelle cried.

That's right. Five rings told everyone to—

Natalie gasped. "We need to get to the flagpole at the center of camp. That's where everyone is supposed to meet if there's ever an emergency."

He nodded. He remembered the drill from back when he was a camper.

The kids set off down the trail with Finn at the head of the line as he and Natalie followed behind.

"What do you think it is?" he asked.

"I don't know. A lost child. Maybe a medical emergency.

It could be anything," she replied when Fish came huffing up the trail.

"It's an all hands-on deck situation," the big man said, turning to jog alongside them.

"What happened?" Natalie asked.

"Your grandparents had a few community service activities planned for the week."

"Okay."

"They'd scheduled a car wash and invited a few community groups to camp."

"Which ones?" Natalie asked.

"The local Elks Club for some fishing, the high school marching band to swim in the cove, and the retired nuns from the convent are here, too," Fish answered, counting off the groups on his fingers.

"Nuns?" Jake repeated.

"Yeah, Hal and Bev open the camp up all the time to the community. Bev does an art class with them," Fish answered.

"What's the problem?" Natalie asked.

Fish slowed to a walk and mopped his brow with a handkerchief. "They were supposed to come on different days this week, but they're all here right now."

"Right now?" Natalie parroted back.

"Right now," the man replied.

"All of them?" she questioned.

"Yep, all of them. And your grandparents aren't here. Your grandpa had an appointment, and then they were going to pick up the lobsters for tonight," Fish replied as they came out of the woods to find complete pandemonium.

"Oh, boy," she said, followed by an overwhelmed sigh as the children continued down the hill and ran into the crowd.

"Jesus, Heels!" he breathed, taking in the hordes of people milling around.

"What should we tell them? Do you think we should wait until your grandparents get back to do anything?" Fish asked.

Natalie shook her head. "No, we have to do something. Fish, try to gather everyone together."

The man nodded, then hurried down the hill.

"Can you do one of those loud whistles, Jake?" she asked.

His gaze bounced between her and the swarm of people milling around. "Yeah."

She grabbed his hand and led him through the crowd over to a bench, then pulled him up with her to stand.

"Okay, do it," she said.

His brows knit together. "What are you going to do?"

She blew out a breath. "Try to get this mess organized."

"How?"

She wrung her hands. "I'm not totally sure, but we've got to do something. I don't want to disappoint these people. Service projects are important to my grandparents. I'd hate for the community to think Camp Woolwich was falling apart."

Was Camp Woolwich falling apart? Hal Woolwich certainly didn't look like he was operating at one hundred percent.

Shit! He couldn't let his mind go there. Not now.

He raised his hand to his mouth. "You ready?"

She nodded. "Do it."

He raised his hand to his mouth and whistled, a loud slicing sound that cut through the crowd, silencing them.

"Wow, you're good at that," Natalie said, wide-eyed.

"I lived on a dairy farm for a while when I was a teenager. This is how I used to call in the cows."

He never spoke of that time, but with her, it just came out.

She nodded, then glanced out at the crowd of frowning faces. "Hello, everyone. There seems to be a little scheduling snafu, but I've got a plan."

"What are you going to do?" Leslie called, dragging Leo with her to the front of the crowd.

Without thinking, Jake took her hand. "You're a teacher, right, Heels?"

"Yeah."

"What would you do if this were a bunch of unruly kids?"

She lifted her chin. "Okay, Woolwich family, we've got guests, and we're going to break into groups to make sure our friends from the community have a lovely time here at Camp Woolwich."

He watched in awe as Natalie divided her family into groups and assigned them each an area. Then, she proceeded to direct the different community organizations to different camp locations. Like a general calling the shots, the masses moved out in military precision.

He watched as the Woolwich teens, usually glued to their phones, led the marching band down to the waterfront. The Elks group set off for the dock to fish while a third Woolwich battalion headed toward the camp's entrance to start washing the cars. She even had a team of family members head over to the dining hall to start on making sandwiches to feed the masses.

She leaned into him as the area around the flagpole cleared out, and he wrapped his arm around her. "I thought you were supposed to be the screw-up Woolwich?"

"I usually am," she answered with a touch of awe to her words when a soft voice caught their attention.

"Dear, where would you like us to go?"

They turned, and he nearly fell off the bench.

"Holy—" he began when Natalie clamped her hand over her mouth and pasted on a smile.

How the heck did they miss a cadre of nuns?

Dressed in habits and veils with their hands clasped in front of them, a half dozen ancient brides of Christ smiled up at them.

"Oh, Sisters, I'm sorry. You're all here for an art class, correct?" Natalie asked as he helped her down from the bench.

"Yes, Beverly usually teaches it. I believe she's your grandmother," the woman replied, then shook Natalie's hand. "I'm Sister Anne, and these are the esteemed retired nuns who reside at the convent in town."

"I'm Natalie, and this is Jake. My grandmother's not here, but I'm an art teacher, and it would be an honor if I could work with you today."

"And him, too," said a pint-sized, wrinkly nun, elbowing her way to the front of the group.

"Behave, Sister Evangeline," Sister Anne warned.

"You want me?" he asked.

"Oh, yes, you!" the nun answered, looking him up and down like a piece of meat.

Natalie threaded her arm with his. "I'm sure Jake would be happy to assist."

He cocked his head to the side. "I would?"

"You would," she answered.

"I don't know anything about art," he said under his breath.

"You can assist me," she said through a pasted-on grin.

"Um, okay," he answered, throwing a glance at the little nun, still eyeing him like a turkey on Thanksgiving.

Natalie gestured to the lodge, and the group headed toward the old building. They entered through a squeaky screen door and were met with the familiar scent of paint and soda pop that permeated the building. The ground floor was essentially a multi-purpose space that served as a place for kids to hang out with ping-pong tables and beanbag chairs scattered around and what looked like the same old Coke vending machine humming along in the corner. He followed the women up the stairs to the second floor that had barely changed in fifteen years. Sunlight streamed in and illuminated stacks of construction paper and rusty coffee cans that housed markers, colored pencils, and an array of rainbow flecked paintbrushes.

He picked up a small sign. "Mistakes and imperfections are part of the process," he said, reading the faded words.

Natalie touched the corner. "It's my grandmother's motto."

"We're all a work in progress," he said, veering from his usual cocksure persona—the facade that hid the boy within.

"We are," she answered, gently, her soothing voice washing over him.

The nuns sat down, and one of the sisters removed a stack of sketch pads from a large tote.

"What were you drawing last time?" Natalie asked, settling herself on a stool at the front of the room.

Sister Anne folded her hands on the table. "The theme has been Adam and Eve in the Garden of Eden. We've been drawing still life, and today—"

"We draw him," the tiny nun, Sister Evangeline, said with her bony finger, pointing his way.

"Me?" he said, then gulped.

Holy Mary! This ninety-year-old sure had plenty of get-up-and-go.

Now it was Natalie's turn to eye him. "You are the only man here, Jake, and if the theme is Adam and Eve, and they came expecting to draw Adam..." she trailed off.

"Christ!" he muttered, then blushed. "I mean, shit! No, that doesn't work either. Crap! That one's okay, right?" he asked, turning to Sister Anne.

The nuns stared at him with their mouths hanging open, except the little one who tossed him a wink.

"I like him," she said, rubbing her wrinkly hands together.

He glanced at the women and then to Natalie. He couldn't let her down.

"Sure, I can be Adam," he said as resolutely as one can when being ogled by a feisty, pint-sized woman of God.

"Adam didn't wear clothes," Sister Evangeline added, undressing him with her eyes.

"Are you sure?" he asked, forgetting who he was talking to.

"Maybe just take off your shirt," Natalie offered.

"My shirt?"

"And the hat," the little nun ordered.

He went up to Natalie, glanced back at the smiling sisters, then bent down to whisper into his fake girlfriend's ear. "Is this normal?"

"I sketched nudes in college. It's not that uncommon," she answered.

"Heels, I think those horny nuns want to see me naked," he whispered back.

"They're not horny nuns." She glanced over his shoulder, then covered her mouth with her hand. "Well, maybe one is, but the rest seem okay."

"Do you think this is funny?" he asked, chancing another glance at the women.

She held back a grin. "It is kind of funny?"

He let out a sigh. "It is kind of funny."

He turned to face the women, then slowly removed his hat and T-shirt.

The little nun's gaze raked over his body. "Now, that's an Adam."

"What's going on in here?"

He whipped around to find Hal and Bev Woolwich standing in the doorway.

Natalie came to his side. "Hi, Grandma and Grandpa. I was going to lead the class in a sketching exercise."

Bev entered the room with a creased brow. "Why is Jake half-naked?"

"Because your theme is Adam and Eve in the Garden of Eden, and we needed an Adam," she answered.

Bev's eyes twinkled, just like Natalie's. "Yes, but we're sketching still life, like apples and other fruits. That's where the Garden of Eden theme came into play."

"You're not sketching nudes?" he asked, throwing a disapproving glare at the brides of Christ who, remarkably, looked quite pleased with themselves.

"Goodness, no," Bev chuckled.

He turned from Bev and met the little nun's eye.

She shrugged. "It was worth a shot."

"We saw Fish downstairs," Bev began addressing the nuns. "Sisters, I'm sorry that the schedule got mixed-up. I'm not sure how it happened."

"It sounds like Natalie saved the day, though," Hal added.

Natalie waved off the praise. "It was nothing. I just told everyone where to go."

The old man's features remained neutral. "No one else stepped up."

"Jake helped, too," she added.

Hal nodded. "How about you get dressed, Jake, and join me while I go check on the Elks Club?"

"I'd be glad to," he replied, then took Natalie's hand. "Unless you need me to stay."

She smiled up at him with a look of such genuine gratitude the breath caught in his throat.

"Oh, we'll be fine, dear. And Natalie can help me teach the sisters the four main shading techniques," Bev answered, retrieving a bowl of oranges from the shelf as Sister Evangeline grumbled.

Natalie squeezed his hand. "I'm good. It'll be nice to teach with my grandmother."

He leaned in and pressed a kiss to her lips. "I'll see you later."

His fake girlfriend released a tiny gasp, clearly not expecting the kiss. They were supposed to be putting up a ruse of being a couple, faking a connection.

But he wasn't pretending.

It felt natural.

Shit.

Hal tapped the doorframe. "Let's head out, Jake. It looks like Bev and Nat have things under control."

"Yes, sir! Absolutely," he answered, whipping on his shirt, then grabbing his hat.

He needed some distance from playing the good boyfriend. That had to be it. They'd spent every moment together since he joined her in line at the airport, which seemed like a lifetime ago.

"Be good, you two," Bev called after them.

He glanced over his shoulder into the art room and

caught Natalie smiling and grazing her fingertips across her lips.

This con was getting complicated.

"Life happens fast here," Hal said, leading him out of the lodge.

"Natalie said each hour feels like a day," he answered, trying without much luck to get her out of his head. He couldn't squander this one-on-one time with Hal. Any information he could glean from the head of the Woolwich family could be imperative in his plan to persuade the man to sell.

"It's more like each hour feels like a month. There's not a lot of bullshit when it comes to life at Camp Woolwich. Time is precious, and the moments here count." The man stopped walking and inhaled a deep breath. "Do you mind if we rest for a second?"

"Sure," he answered and stared at the waterfront, teeming with kids swimming and splashing as a pair of Sunfish sailboats bobbed with the current.

"Do you sail?" Hal asked.

He shook his head. "Not anymore."

"I see," the man replied.

"It's beautiful here," he said, hoping to shift the conversation away from himself.

"You'd know a thing or two about that, wouldn't you, Mr. Teller?"

The breath caught in his throat. "I don't understand what you mean, Hal."

"You're in real estate, right?" the man pressed, then gestured for them to start walking.

Dammit!

Hal chuckled. "It's not a bad thing, Jake. I heard it through the Woolwich grapevine. You must have mentioned it at breakfast."

Jake's gaze dropped to the ground. "I didn't think anyone was listening."

Hal glanced at him. "You're the newcomer, Natalie's Jake. Everyone is interested."

Natalie's Jake.

What would this man think if he learned he wasn't? But he couldn't go there. He'd cross that bridge when he had to —after the deal was done. Now, he had to brush all thoughts of Natalie Callahan aside and transition into sales mode.

He schooled his features. "That's right. I work in commercial real estate."

"What do you think of our little slice of Maine?" Hal asked, gesturing to the coastline.

"I think you're in possession of some valuable real estate," he answered, relaxing into the song and dance of talking shop.

Hal nodded. "Do you have a number in your head?"

Jake stilled. That caught him off guard.

"Off the top of my head?" he asked, doing his best to hide the surprise in his voice.

"Sure," Hal answered, crossing his arms as if they were simply discussing the price of a carton of eggs and not the value of the man's life's work.

"Ten, maybe fifteen," he replied, pretending to come up with a number.

The dance had begun, and he always started low.

Hal raised an eyebrow. "Ten or fifteen million?"

Jake nodded. "With the cove and access to the ocean, not to mention the wildlife preserve, I'd say that your land is worth a substantial amount of money."

"Hmm," the man hummed, staring across the cove and giving him the New Englander non-answer.

"Are you considering any alternative plans for the land?" he asked, choosing his words carefully. There was an art to closing a deal, and that started with planting the seed. In the end, if he'd done his job right, Hal and Bev would believe that they were the ones who came up with the idea to sell.

"We've had forty-three Woolwich weddings here over the years. Lara and Leslie were the only two who chose to get married somewhere else." He gestured to the water. "I taught my children and grandchildren how to fish right off that dock, and Natalie sailed to Woolwich Island all by herself in that very Sunfish when she was twelve years old."

Jake stared at the small sailboat and swallowed back memories of sailing with his parents. He'd lean over the side and drag his fingers along the glassy surface of Lake Michigan as they set a course to the Beaver Islands or over to Fish Creek. But just as the thought materialized, years of compartmentalizing allowed him to tuck it away.

That carefree boy had died along with his parents.

He kept his features neutral. "I'm sure this place holds many memories for you."

Hal's lips twisted into a knowing half grin. "I'm sensing a but."

This man was no fool.

"But things change. Priorities change," he offered.

"Is that how you see it?" Hal pressed.

How did he see it?

Before Natalie Callahan crashed into his life, he believed that wholeheartedly. There were no constants in this world, and the only person he could count on was himself. Never get sentimental—and don't become attached to a place, even somewhere as magical as this. But now, he didn't see dollar signs when he gazed out at the water. He saw eyes. Natalie's eyes. Green and sparkling. People always talk about the ocean blue, but here, gazing out to where the ocean spanned across the horizon, he was met with an endless watery blanket of deep green.

Natalie green.

They continued down the path in silence, passing the boathouse and headed toward the dock where several of the Woolwich grandkids sat with fishing poles alongside members of the Elks Club.

Hal jiggled the weathered wooden post leading out to the dock and frowned.

"I bet there's a decent amount of maintenance to keep a place like this going," Jake said, dropping a few more bread-crumbs. He had to stick to his plan and surreptitiously guide the conversation toward selling. The kiss keeper bombshell had thrown him off track. But Natalie was done with Jakes, and he knew better than anyone that he couldn't give her what she deserved. And, he could not forget what was on the line.

Control. Total and complete control of his life.

"I won't lie to you, Jake. There is a hell of a lot of upkeep, but it's a labor of love," Hal said, breaking into his thoughts.

"Well, fifty years in one place is a long time," he replied, continuing the song and dance he was so well versed in, but that damn bothersome tightness was back in his chest.

Hal cocked his head to the side and observed him closely. "Can I give you a piece of advice, Jake?"

"Sure," he answered

Hal held his gaze. "It doesn't feel like a long time if you're with the right person. And once you find that person, you've got to be smart enough and brave enough to surrender control and give up your heart."

"That seems like a lot to risk," he replied.

Hal gave him a knowing look. "Ah, but imagine what you would gain."

He stared out at the water as the breeze picked up, and he heard her name—*Natalie Callahan*—whispered on the breeze.

"What did you gain?" he asked.

"A lifetime of love and happiness, and that, Mr. Teller, is very difficult to put a price on," Hal said, clapping him on the shoulder before heading down the weathered dock.

Jake watched the great-grandkids cluster around Hal, holding up their catches for him to admire, then turned his attention back to the water. His phone pinged, but he ignored it and stared at a sailboat in the distance. A boat not so different than the one his parents used to have. It rocked gently in the Natalie green sea, and a lightness took over. A lightness that never accompanied closing a deal or checking his robust bank account balance. A strange sensation he hadn't known in years until it hit him, and he knew what he had to do.

"What do you think, Aunt Nat?"

Natalie glanced up to find Josie and Maddie twirling in circles in the center of the lodge as their homemade Hawaiian skirts, made not with grass but strips of fabric sporting tiny lobsters, fluttered around their legs.

She finished cutting a strip of fabric, handed it off to one of her aunts, then grinned at the children. "They're perfect! You both look ready for the lobster luau."

"Why do we do a lobster luau?" Annabelle asked, shimmying around the table in her own little makeshift skirt.

"Good question," Leslie said under her breath, weaving her way to sit in the corner with her sister through the room of Woolwich women working on their Maine inspired Hawaiian costumes.

But not even Leslie could dampen her mood. She'd done it. Natalie Callahan, the screwup Woolwich granddaughter, had turned a scheduling melee into an event to remember. Elks had caught buckets of trout, cars had been washed, the band got in a fun-filled afternoon on the waterfront, and the nuns had sketched. Their guest had left camp smiling, except for Sister Evangeline, who had a thing for Jake. She sported a scowl for the entire lesson and had bucked practicing shading techniques on fruit to sketch Jake's torso. If there were one thing she could say about the feisty nun, it was that the old gal still had an excellent memory and had produced one heck of a drawing.

But she hadn't earned this victory alone. A delicious shiver traveled down her spine and settled low in her belly at the thought of Jake, taking her hand, threading his fingers with hers, and standing by her side. And then her mind wandered to her fake boyfriend's body, shirtless with every ripped muscle exposed, and she couldn't blame the nun one bit for lamenting his absence. Those abs, the same abs that had pressed against her back as he took her from behind this morning, were seared into her memory as well. But it wasn't only his spectacular body that she missed.

She missed him.

She hadn't seen Jake since they parted in the art room earlier in the day. Her grandfather had whisked him away to go fishing and, most likely, had him on lobster bake duty with the rest of the Woolwich men and boys as if he were hers, and a real part of all this Woolwich family madness.

The strange thing about this ruse, this con, was that the lines had blurred. Sure, they'd had the greatest sex of her life last night, but that had been predicated on intercourse simply being intercourse—a transaction between two willing people. A transaction like a man pretending to be a woman's boyfriend.

But this morning, when they were half-awake, not consumed with playing a part and only relying on touch and desire, it had felt real. And after that, when she'd led him up to the well and shared her kiss keeper curse story, it was as if every cell in her body had ached for his kiss—as if the well or the ghosts of Otis Wiscasset and Muriel Boothe demanded it. Or maybe it was her yearning, her body begging to be touched by this man who'd gone from a complete stranger to her lover in the space of hardly more than a day. Still, when they'd nearly kissed at the well, and he'd gazed into her eyes, she would have sworn that she'd glimpsed a flash of wonder and an intense longing that took her breath away.

Could what had started as a parlor trick parlayed into something more, or was this her artist's heart leading her astray with another Jake, again? The way he worked her body, no, worshipped her body, had to mean something. She closed her eyes, remembering the sweet slide of their bodies as he thrust his big, hard—

"Aunt Nat? Are you okay?"

Natalie blinked. "Sorry, I was just thinking about..."

"Kissing Uncle Jake?" Josie said with a giggle as she, Maddie, and Annabelle twirled about.

And licking his torso all the way down to his magical cock, but she was in charge of the kids and needed to keep this PG.

"You wanted to know about the luau, right, Annabelle?" she asked, forcing herself to switch gears.

"Yeah!" the little girl cried and wiggled onto her lap.

She smoothed the strips of Annabelle's skirt then waved in Josie and Maddie. "The lobster bake luau is a tradition that started a long time ago, right after Mimi and Poppy opened Camp Woolwich. Every year, the girls all gather in the lodge to create their costumes while the boys take care of the lobster bake preparations on the beach."

"Why can't the girls do the lobster bake preparations?" Josie asked.

"That's a good question! It's always been this way, but

that doesn't mean it can't change. I might bring that up with Mimi," she answered.

"Bring what up with Mimi?" her grandmother asked, entering the room with a crate of bright yellow hibiscus flowers.

"Josie and I were thinking that someday the girls should be in charge of the lobster bake beach prep, and the boys can make lobster skirts."

"I like it! A little change could be good for Camp Woolwich," her grandmother answered.

"What are all the flowers for?" Annabelle asked.

"These are for our hair," her grandmother said, sliding one into Annabelle's dark locks. "And for the leis."

"Leis?" the child parroted back.

"They're flower necklaces that you get to give to someone special," her grandmother answered, pulling out several flowers then passing off the crate to a Woolwich cousin.

"Can I give one to Finn?" the little girl asked.

"Sure," Natalie answered. Growing up, she'd always made a lei for her grandfather or for Fish, but she'd never given one to a boyfriend—even a fake boyfriend.

"I thought you were supposed to give a lei to somebody you love," Maddie chirped, her cheeks turning pink.

Annabelle scrunched up her face in a confused pout. "I love Finn. He's my cousin."

"Gross!" Maddie and Josie cried in unison.

Annabelle cocked her head to the side. "Why's it gross?"

"It's not gross. It's perfectly fine to love your cousin, sweetheart," her grandmother answered.

"Are you going to give one to Jake?" Josie asked.

"Do you love him?" Maddie pressed.

Love him? She hardly knew him, but that didn't stop the flutter in her belly at the mention of his name.

"I certainly like him an awful lot," she answered, feeling her cheeks heat.

It wasn't a lie.

"He's very handsome," her grandmother added.

"And he can climb trees, Mimi," Annabelle supplied.

The hint of a smile pulled at the corners of her grandmother's lips. "An admirable quality, indeed," the woman answered, then clapped her hands to get everyone's attention. "Ladies, the flowers have arrived. Let's get started on those leis."

Natalie went to work, and the room buzzed with conversations as the women strung flowers and made final additions to their skirts when her grandmother sat down next to her.

"He cares for you," she said, sliding a bloom into her hair.

"Who?" Natalie asked, keeping her eyes on the lei. If anyone could read her, it was her grandma Bev.

"Jake, who else, sweetheart?" her grandmother answered, handing her a flower.

Natalie took the bloom and slid it into her hair. She needed to change the subject. It was one thing to parade her fake boyfriend around camp. It was a whole other bag of wax to lie to her grandmother's face.

"I'm glad you and Grandpa have gathered us here to celebrate your fiftieth anniversary. I've missed this place so much."

Bev threaded a flower onto a string. "You found your artist roots here many moons ago."

"I did, thanks to you," she replied. It was like old times,

creating art alongside her grandmother, even if it was only a lei.

Her grandmother stroked one of the hibiscus petals. "Oh, no. I may have guided you in that direction, but you've always had the artist's spark. That gift to see the beauty in everything and everyone."

Natalie glanced over at Leslie and Lara, both women glued to their phones, then turned her attention back to her grandmother.

"I don't know if I see the beauty in everything, but you and Grandpa have never look at me like I'm a..." she trailed off.

Bev set down the lei. "A what?"

"A failure," she answered.

Her grandmother's brows knit together. "Is that how you see yourself?"

Natalie sighed. "Well, I've got no job and no boy—" she stopped herself. "You must know that I lost another job. I texted it to Mom, and then it hit the Woolwich stratosphere."

"Maybe it happened for a reason. You never know when opportunity will come knocking on your door," her grandmother said with a twinkle in her eyes.

Natalie squeezed the woman's hand. "How do you stay so optimistic? After all the years running Camp Woolwich, it couldn't have always been easy."

"Oh, it wasn't, but the universe led me to your grandfather and brought us to this place. So, I'd say I'm pretty lucky," her grandmother replied.

"And I'd agree."

The women startled at the voice behind them.

"What are you doing in here, Hal?" her grandmother asked.

"I'm here to escort the prettiest girl to the luau," he said, taking her grandmother's hand.

"What about me?" Annabelle pouted.

"I meant the two prettiest girls," he answered, scooping up the little girl in his other arm.

"Are you sure you've got her?" her grandmother asked, eyeing her husband.

"I'm fine, Bev," he answered gently, then made Annabelle laugh with a silly face.

"All right, Woolwich women, let's head over to the lobster bake luau," her grandma Bev announced.

"Are you coming, Aunt Nat?" Josie called over her shoulder.

Natalie glanced around. She could use a Woolwich-free minute to collect herself. "I'm going to tidy up a little in here. I won't be long."

The room cleared out as she went table to table, brushing loose petals and wisps of fabric into her hand, soaking in all the time she'd spent in this room, then stilled, sensing Jake was there. She grinned as the heat returned to her cheeks.

"Are you just going to watch?" she said over her shoulder as the door to the lodge let out a weary creak and gently closed.

"Wow! You look..." Jake began.

She dusted the remains of the lobster luau prep into the bin then turned. "Silly?" she asked, staring down at her feet.

Why was she so nervous all of a sudden?

"No, stunning," he finished.

"In a tank top and a lobster skirt?" she teased.

Jake crossed the room as if he owned it, and she couldn't stop her pulse from racing at the sight of him. But before he could reach her, he stopped and frowned.

"What?" she asked.

"It's your feet," he answered, concern lacing the words.

"What about them?" She wiggled her toes.

"You're wearing sandals, Heels."

The mention of his nickname for her sent an electric jolt of anticipation through her body.

"It's a luau," she answered, doing her best to not look like an enamored idiot.

He raised a finger. "It's a *lobster bake* luau. And I've been working my ass off for the last few hours, digging a hole big enough to fit enough lobsters to feed your entire family, and..."

"And what?" she tossed back, her hands on her hips.

He raised an eyebrow. "And if I can see your feet, you know who else will be able to see them."

She grinned. "It'll be dark soon, and I can guard my toes against Dr. Foot Fetish. Plus, I think you've put the fear of God into him, and that doesn't hurt."

"He's not so bad," Jake said with a shrug.

Her jaw dropped. "Leo?"

"Yeah, I spent the day fishing with your grandpa and the Elks Club. Leo and Marcus were with us. When your cousins aren't around, their husbands aren't too bad. Marcus did try to eat the bait, but we got him squared away with a bag of Funyuns."

"So, you survived?" she asked with a chuckle.

His expression softened. "You mean, did your grandfather grill his favorite granddaughter's new Jake? A little bit, but I survived."

"You seem to be able to handle yourself. It's almost as if you came into this whole ruse with a plan," she added, trying to get a laugh out of him, but the opposite happened.

Jake's jovial expression faded as the door to the lodge swung open, and Josie and Maddie burst into the room.

"You're the queen, Aunt Nat," they cried as they ran up and handed a crown decked with mini plastic lobsters glued to the side.

She turned to Jake. "How did I become the queen?"

"I nominated you," he answered, but his smile didn't reach his eyes.

The lobster queen was no queen.

"Do you know what the queen has to do?" she asked.

He shrugged. "I figured you'd have to wear that lobster crown. It sounded fun."

"And the queen has to kiss the winner of the blindfolded obstacle course," she added.

"What?" he threw back, his eyes as wide as saucers.

"Didn't you see the obstacle course on the beach?" she pressed.

He shifted his weight. "I figured it was for the kids."

"No, the guys compete, and my grandmother's always been the Lobster Queen."

"I forgot," Jake answered, running his hands through his dark tangle of hair.

She watched him closely as that weird déjà vu thing between them returned.

He shook his head. "I mean, I didn't realize."

"Better hurry! It's about to start," the girls said with a squeal as the screen door slammed behind them.

Natalie paced the length of the room. "One of the older boys will most likely win, and it is only a kiss on the cheek."

"Or it could be Marcus with onion breath or Leo, and he may fake you out and try to kiss your feet," Jake added with a half-laugh half-grimace.

"Ew! That's an awful thing to imagine," she cried.

"Probably not awful for Leo," he said, biting back a grin.

She donned the lobster crown and took his hand, dragging him out of the lodge. "You got me into this, and now I'm going to help you get me out of it."

"How? I don't think the lobster queen has any real powers. Unless that fancy lobster crown lets you command all those cooked lobsters to come to your defense."

"You're awful, and I'm a vegetarian. I'd never rule over dead seafood," she laughed.

"No, that's perfect! Zombie lobsters, coming back from the dead to defend their non-lobster eating queen," he said, lowering his voice as if he were narrating a horror movie.

She shook her head. "Enough with the lobster! You need to focus. The last thing I want to do is kiss Leo or Marcus—even if it is only on the cheek. You nominated me to be queen, so you have to win."

"Because you want to kiss me?" he asked with a cocky twist to his lips.

She shot him a sharp look. "So, I don't have to kiss a perverted podiatrist."

He shrugged. "Fair enough, but how hard can it be to win an obstacle course race?"

"Harder than you think. It's a blindfolded obstacle course, but I'll guide you through it."

"What's up with blindfolds and this place?" he murmured as they headed toward the lobster bake luau on the far end of the camp's coastal property.

"You're about to find out," she said, swiping one off a folding table, then assessed the situation.

Leo and Marcus stood in the crowd of Woolwich men waiting to compete in the race with their heads bent over, having what looked like a serious tête-à-tête with Leslie and Lara.

Jake gestured to the mass of men. "Why does everyone do this? Wait, don't tell me. It's a Woolwich tradition."

"That, and you get the first lobster," she replied.

"Early access lobster and a kiss from the lobster queen. I see the appeal, but why would Leslie and Lara want their husbands to do it?" he asked.

Natalie shook her head. "Because for some reason, Leslie lives to one-up me, and that means also beating you since you're my..."

He frowned. "Yeah, I should have thought about that."

She fashioned the bandana into a blindfold. "It's no use now. I've been crowned. Are you ready?"

"Last call! All the gents who want to get in on the race need to line up!" announced one of the Woolwich uncles.

She turned to her fake boyfriend. "Just today, we've saved a full-bladdered child from peeing his pants in a tree, organized a scheduling nightmare, and thwarted a group of horny nuns. I think we can handle an obstacle course. Plus, you're built like a..."

His lips curved back into that smirk of a smile. "Built like a what?"

She scoffed. "Give me a break! You saw what you did to those women of God! You're like that snake in the Garden of Eden—but with better abs."

"I don't think snakes have abs, Heels."

"You know what I mean." She narrowed her gaze but couldn't hold back a grin.

"On your marks!" her grandmother called from the starting line.

"Hurry, we don't have much time," she said as they weaved their way through the spectators to get to the starting line, edging in next to Leo and Leslie.

Leo glanced at her feet. "It's nice to see you in something other than high heels."

"Oh, shut your trap, Leo, and pay attention!" Leslie snapped, pulling the bandana over her husband's eyes.

"Get set!"

Natalie pushed up onto her tiptoes, and Jake leaned in. "There are four obstacles. You've got the Hula hoop hop, the cone maze, a big jump over a seaweed pit, then you have to cross the length of a giant log and finally, ring the bell."

"Got it," he answered as she pulled the blindfold over his eyes.

"Listen for my voice," she directed.

"Don't worry. I would know your voice anywhere, Heels."

She stared at her blindfolded fake boyfriend. That was a weird thing for him to say, but she didn't have time to mull it over.

"Go!" her grandmother called.

With the awkwardness of twenty blindfolded individuals jostling for the lead, the Woolwich men lurched forward in a tangle of limbs and curse words muttered under their breaths. Lucky for her, Jake broke free of the pack.

"Hula hoops, five paces ahead! Hop, hop, hop!" she called as he approached the first obstacle.

Jake sailed through the hoops, dropping his feet inside the prostrate rings with laser precision.

"Cone maze, straight ahead," she directed. "Two steps right. Four steps left."

Jake wove his way through the narrow passage as if he were Luke Skywalker, and she was the Force, guiding him seamlessly through the battalion of cones.

"What's next?" Jake asked.

"You're going to sprint, and then I'll tell you when to

jump. This is the obstacle that disqualifies most competitors."

Jake bounced back and forth on the balls of his feet. "Where are the podiatrists?"

"Right here!" Leo cried, limbs flailing as he shot forward.

"Run, Jake! Run!" she ordered.

Like a thoroughbred champing at the bit, Jake took off. In the blink of an eye, he passed Leo and charged toward the mound of slippery seaweed. If he got caught here, it would be over. She'd seen many a Woolwich man thwarted by the slimy substance. She sprinted along the edge of the course with her gaze locked on Jake, timing his steps.

"Jump!" she cried as time seemed to compress and morphed into slow motion.

Jake leaned forward and pushed off just as Leo came up behind him. The two men hung in the air for a split second before Jake's left foot landed on solid ground while Leo came up short, and the seaweed claimed its first casualty. With a thud, the podiatrist fell to the ground, knocking into Marcus. Both men flopped around in the slick greenish-brown pit like a pair of flounder on dry land.

She jumped up and down. "Run, Jake! Foot patrol is out of commission! All you have to do is cross the log."

She glanced over her shoulder at the growing seaweed pile-up. Wives called out to their blindfolded husbands, trying to help them navigate the messy commotion when Leo clawed his way out. Strips of salty seaweed clung to his legs as Leslie yelled for him to run.

This wasn't over yet.

"Where's the log?" Jake asked, running in a zigzag with Leo gaining on him.

"Three paces to the left, then freeze!"

Jake edged over as his toes scuffed the log.

"I need you to channel your inner gymnast. Step up onto the log," she directed.

Leo was closing in, but she couldn't lose her cool. If he fell off, he'd have to start over, and they didn't have a second to waste.

"Follow my voice and take it nice and slow," she called as Leslie ran to her side.

"Get him, Leo! Jake's only a few steps ahead of you. Knock his ass off the trunk and win this thing!" her cousin cried.

"Hurry, Jake!" she called.

The log rolled side to side as the men traversed the knotty trunk. Jake held out his arms for balance.

"How many more steps, Heels?"

She sized up the log. "Five or six!"

Leslie cupped her hands around her mouth to amplify her shrill voice. "Roll the log, Leo! Knock him off!"

"But if I do that, I'll fall off," the man complained, working to keep his balance.

"Do it!" Leslie bellowed.

Leo leaned over, pushing off the side of the log and causing it to roll out of position.

Natalie gasped as Jake hit the end. "Jump off," she cried as Leo crashed to the ground for a second time.

"Where's the bell?" he asked, landing solidly on the ground.

She ran over to the table where the bell sat, waiting for the winner. "Here! It's here!"

"Keep talking, Heels!"

"Keep talking. Okay, here goes. A, B, C, D, E, F, G," she sang out.

Jake bumped into the table.

"Oh, sorry! Stop!" she directed, a second too late. "The bell's right in front of you."

"And Leo?" he asked.

She craned her neck to see past him. "He's on the ground inspecting his foot. He's out for the count. Now, ring the bell!"

Jake patted the table then found the bell's handle. "You know this means that you'll have to kiss me."

She checked on Leo, then spied Marcus, coming in hot. "I know! I know! Hurry! Mr. Funyun Breath is almost to the log!"

"I've never kissed a lobster queen before," he mused as if she wasn't in grave danger of having to kiss not only another idiot doctor but a doctor with a predilection for noshing on bait.

"Ring the damn bell," she said, laughing.

Thank God, the man complied. The clang of the old bell cut through the cheers and chants. Jake peeled off the bandana as a wide grin stretched across his face. "Did you ever doubt me?"

She stared into his eyes—the eyes of a man she hardly knew, yet she could barely remember what life was like before he got in line behind her at the airport.

"No, I never doubted you," she answered, unable to look away.

He straightened her crown. "I'm ready to claim that kiss."

"You don't want to eat your lobster first?" she teased.

His gaze darkened. "Hell no."

She glanced around to find her entire family watching them, then leaned in and lowered her voice. "Remember, we have to make this look—"

Before she could say *real*, Jake cupped her face in his

hands and planted one hell of a kiss on her lips. She wrapped her arms around his neck, and he lifted her feet off the ground as their kiss picked up steam. His grip tightened around her waist as their tongues met in a slow, sensual rhythm. His teeth grazed her bottom lip, and she sighed, again, losing herself to his scent and taste and touch, ready to surrender to her growing desire when someone cleared their throat.

She pulled back a fraction to find her grandfather biting back a grin.

"About done there, claiming your kiss?" he asked.

"Yes, sir," Jake answered, setting her down, then took a step back.

"That was some kiss," her grandmother added, threading her arm with her husband.

"They do that," Lara chimed.

Marcus nodded. "Yeah, you should have seen them last night."

"You should have heard them last night," Leo mumbled.

She glanced up at Jake, then pasted on a beauty queen, or in her case, a lobster queen-sized grin. "Congratulations on your obstacle course win, Jake Teller. Would you like your crustacean?"

For a beat, nobody moved or said a word. Yes, she sounded like a moron. But what was she supposed to say with her family staring at her, all slack-jawed? Thanks for that amazing kiss? It's too bad that my grandpa is hovering a few feet away or else we could have totally gone at it right here on the beach?

"Let's hold off on the lobster for a minute, Nat. I've got a few things I'd like to announce," her grandfather said, sharing a look with her grandmother.

"Is everything okay, Grandpa?" Lara asked.

"That all depends on one of you," her grandmother answered.

"One of us," Lara and Leslie echoed.

"Your grandmother and I have spent fifty wonderful years here at Camp Woolwich. We've raised our children here and welcomed friends, cousins, grandchildren, and nieces and nephews. But we've come to a turning point."

"And as much as we love Camp Woolwich, we're getting older, and there are some things on our bucket list we'd like to do while we still can. So, tonight, we're announcing that we're ready to pass the torch, and we're hoping that one of you will accept," her grandmother said, smiling into the crowd.

"You want one of us to take over?" Natalie asked. She'd known something was up with her grandparents, but never in her wildest dreams would she have imagined they'd give up the camp.

"Wouldn't it make more sense to sell the land since no one in the family has followed in your footsteps? There's nobody among us that could drop everything to run a camp," Leslie replied.

Bev nodded. "That's true. We never expected any of our children or grandchildren to follow in the family business. We wanted you all to have your own lives and follow your own passions."

Her grandfather nodded. "We've looked into several options, but Bev and I know it's time to take a step back. We're seventy-five years old, but I'll be damned to sell this place to a stranger before trying to keep it in the family," her grandfather added.

The crowd buzzed with chatter as people shook their heads and crossed their arms.

Natalie glanced away from the group and stared up at

the camp. The setting sun lit the buildings in a warm glow. She'd seen it like this a thousand times, maybe more. It had become a constant, grounding force in her life. A memory that she clung to when her life was falling apart. Not only that, it didn't seem possible that Camp Woolwich could cease to exist. It was a pillar of the community. They offered summer camp scholarships to foster children and constantly invited community groups to enjoy the grounds.

But more than that, this place was her center.

The one place where she fit, where she belonged. For much of her youth, she'd been shuttled back and forth across the country. Two bedrooms. Two lives—one as her mother's daughter and the other as her father's little girl. Here, at Camp Woolwich, she was herself, her best self, her whole self.

"Are you okay, Heels?" Jake asked, pressing his hand to the small of her back.

She looked up at him and saw pain and confusion welling in his gaze. Why would this affect him so profoundly?

"Here's what it comes down to, folks," her grandfather said, cutting into the conversations and drawing everyone's attention. "Bev and I can sell, and we can all share in the profits or someone—"

Natalie shook her head. "No, we're not selling. I'll do it. I want to run Camp Woolwich."

"Do you think you can handle it?" her grandfather asked.

She swallowed past the lump in her throat. "I do."

"Hold on a second," Leslie quipped. "You guys are going to trust our family's legacy to Natalie? She's been fired more times than I can count, and she bounces around from guy to guy—and only seems to date men named Jake—which is pretty damn weird. Plus, let's face it. She's not reliable, and she wouldn't be a good steward of all you've built."

"Yeah," Lara chimed. "How can she take over? She doesn't even eat lobster!"

"Nor does she care for her feet properly," Leo mumbled.

Leslie stepped forward with her signature bullshit sincere expression shellacked to her face. "Grandma, Grandpa, I love the camp, but I fear that Natalie would run this place into the ground."

Jake took a step forward and started to say something, but she stopped him.

"This isn't your battle," she said, giving his hand a squeeze. She turned to her cousin and lifted her chin. "You know what, Leslie? I don't know what I ever did to you. We were close once, but then you changed, and you've been awful to me ever since. You've teased me, tricked me, and you seem to take great pleasure in all my failures."

Her cousin's jaw dropped, but Natalie wasn't done. A switch had flipped, and little Natalie Callahan, the youngest Woolwich grandchild, was done taking shit.

She climbed up onto the folding table and stared out at her family as a resolve like nothing she'd ever known coursed through her veins.

"I know what you all think of me, but I have news for you. I love this place. With or without your support, I'm going to continue building on what Grandma and Grandpa have created. In fact, I'm going to make it better. There are going to be more nuns, more Elks, more marching bands, and I'll double camp attendance. I'm not going to stand back and watch Camp Woolwich become condos or a beach resort. This place is a part of me—part of us—and I'm going to make sure it stays a part of our family."

She met her grandfather's eye, and he winked. He actually winked.

Holy shit!

He was onboard. He was okay with this.

The reality of the situation hit her like a ton of bricks.

She took a steadying breath. "Now, if you'll excuse me. I have a lot of planning and whatnot to get to. So, as the lobster luau queen and soon to be camp owner, I bid you to enjoy your murdered lobsters," she added, then jumped off the table and sprinted up the beach.

The salt air rushed over her skin and blew off her lobster queen crown as she ran.

What did she do? Could she even run a camp? And did she agree to move here permanently?

"Jesus, Heels. That was..."

She glanced over her shoulder as her fake boyfriend ran up alongside her.

She waved him off and kept going, knowing where she needed to go to work all this out.

"Natalie, can you stop for one second?" he called.

She stilled and caught her breath. "I get it, Jake. That was kind of insane, but I couldn't let this place go. I couldn't let it get sold off because that's exactly what my cousins or any other family member would do. You get it, don't you? This place gives people..."

"Hope," he answered.

She blew out a tight breath, then spotted what she'd headed up the beach to find. "Yes, that's it exactly, but now, I need to think. I may have made the craziest decision of my life, and I have to figure this out on my own." She touched his chest as the last wisps of light warmed his features. "As sweet as you've been, agreeing to play the part of my boyfriend, and God help me, the sex has been mind-blowing, but I need to be alone, and I need to work this out all on my own because we both know that, at the end of the day, you're just another Jake who's going to leave me."

She turned away from him and stared out at the water, listening to the ocean. The unbroken ebb and flow she could never forget, night after summer night, falling asleep to its calming lullaby when Jake came up behind her and whispered in her ear.

"What if I'm not the Jake who leaves?"

9

Sweet Jesus! He'd said it—said he wanted to be her Jake, her real Jake. And he knew he'd spoken the words because Natalie's jaw had nearly dropped to the sandy beach.

She closed her mouth, shook her head, then headed toward a cluster of bushy pines, casting long shadows in the setting sun.

"I don't think you know what you're saying," she whispered over the sound of the water.

But he did. He knew exactly what he was saying. After his conversation with Hal, it had all become crystal clear. Staring out at the vast ocean of Natalie green waters, it seemed so simple. He'd lost his way. He'd forgotten what mattered. But there was a way out of his empty life, and it was right in front of him.

Choose hope.

Choose love.

Choose Natalie.

She was his kiss keeper. Since he was a boy, she was the constant reminder that there was good in the world, and now he had a chance to be with her—to be loved and to give love, real love like what his parents had shared.

He and Natalie had a spark from the moment they met. A connection that bound them together. He knew it every time he touched her, and she felt it, too. He could see it in her eyes each time she smiled at him.

He wasn't just another Jake to her.

But, holy shit! What was he supposed to do now? She'd volunteered to take over the camp. The very camp he was tasked with acquiring.

His thoughts spiraled as he tried to piece it all together.

Did his conversation with Hal set in motion this idea to offer the camp to his family? And not in a million years would he have imagined that Natalie would volunteer to run the show all by herself. But isn't this what he wanted—to have her and to be able to experience the magic of Camp Woolwich?

He wanted to come clean and tell who he was and what he was really doing there, but now, with her taking over, what would she think of his con? Her ruse had been so innocent. She merely wanted her family to think she had it together. But his deception meant uprooting everything she loved and stealing the camp out from under her family.

He couldn't tell her—at least, not until he could figure out what the hell to do with Charlie. And what was up with his boss? Text after text, asking for updates. It was like the guy was obsessed with this place. Then, as if the old man could sense it, his damn phone chimed an incoming text.

He pulled his phone and, sure enough, it was from his boss.

Where's my update? I expect an answer.

He shook his head and pocketed his cell. When he

looked up, he found Natalie tugging a weathered, half-beaten to hell rowboat from behind a cluster of trees.

"What are you doing with that?" he asked.

She looked down at the old boat. "Not flying."

He glanced at the calm waters, glittering with the last rays of sunlight. "It's getting late. The sun's almost set. You can't take that thing out on the water."

She dragged the boat past him and edged it into the ocean. "I know this coastline like the back of my hand, Jake. I need to think, and being on the water helps me put things into perspective."

But he needed to keep her on dry land because he had to talk to her.

"You shouldn't steal that boat, Heels."

She chuckled. "I'm not stealing it. It belongs to Fish, and I promise you, he won't mind if I borrow it."

He took a step toward her. "Natalie, I meant what I said."

She adjusted the oars then froze. "Jake, if you hadn't noticed, my life just dramatically changed. I need some time on the water," she replied, not meeting his gaze.

With one last pull, the rowboat pitched forward then rocked in the shallow waters. Steadying the boat, Natalie climbed in and settled herself on the center bench.

He paced the shore. "Where's your lifejacket?"

"Right here," she said, holding up a pair of sagging orange floatation devices. "Two to choose from."

She strapped one on, then gripped the oars, but he couldn't let her go. His gaze bounced wildly between the little boat and the vast expanse of water. The same waters that had taken his parents. But he wasn't about to lose Natalie, too. She needed to understand that he was all in. And that started by getting his ass in that rickety as hell boat.

Sprinting through the salty water, he caught up to the tiny boat, gripped the bow, and hoisted himself into the creaky vessel.

"I didn't think you did water," she said unblinking.

He glanced from side to side as the boat evened out. "I don't. But I also don't do commitment or relationships, but here I am."

She rested her head on the handle of the oar. "Jake, you don't have to be here."

He stroked her cheek. "I don't think you understand how much I do."

"You can't understand," she said with a shake of her head.

He leaned forward. "I know how important Camp Wool-wich is to you. It's important to me, too. You're important to me. Can't you see, we're good together, Heels, and I never thought I'd find you."

She frowned. "Find me? We've only just met."

The rowboat drifted in the current, and he strapped on the other lifejacket.

Shit! He couldn't screw this up, but that meant walking a fine line.

"Find someone like you. Someone who filled the part of my heart that I thought would always remain a gaping hole," he replied. It wasn't a lie, but it also wasn't the whole truth.

Her features softened. "Is that why you don't do water? Did you have a bad experience?"

He closed his eyes and focused on the rhythmic sway of the boat. A sensation that used to be a comfort. He could almost hear his parents, chatting quietly, as he drifted off to sleep in their trim little Herreshoff sailboat.

He rubbed his hands on his thighs and released a tight

breath. "Yes, I lost my parents in a sailing accident when I was thirteen. I grew up on the lake in northern Michigan. My mom and dad were both solid sailors, but they were in unfamiliar waters and, a storm came in."

She took his hand into hers. "Were you with them?"

He swallowed hard. "No, I wasn't there. It was just the two of them. They were on a special trip, celebrating their anniversary, and I was..." he trailed off and stared at the land —at where he'd been, safe at Camp Woolwich, while his mother and father drowned out at sea.

"Oh, Jake. I'm so sorry," she said, filling in the silence and saving him from telling her the whole story.

He nodded. "After that, my life changed completely. My parents had me late in life. My grandparents passed before I was born, and my mom and dad didn't come from large families. My uncle, my dad's brother, took me in. He wasn't happy about it. For the next five years, I worked my ass off on his dairy farm after school, and he never let me forget that I was a financial burden to him. The day I turned eighteen, I left and never looked back. I thought that making money, lots of money, would make me feel complete and fill that damn hole in my heart. I never wanted to rely on anyone but myself ever again."

Natalie stared out at the water. "I know a thing or two about wanting to feel complete. That's why I can't let the camp get sold off. This is the only place where I feel whole. I love my parents, don't get me wrong, but after they divorced, I became secondary to their careers—a part-time daughter. But when I'm here, I know who I am. I—"

His phone chimed, and she released his hand and sat back. "You can get that if you need to."

He slid the phone out to find another message from

Charlie, and all he wanted was to be free. "I don't need to check anything. In fact, I'm done with that part of my life."

"Done with making buckets of money?" she asked.

He nodded, then chucked the phone into the ocean.

Natalie gasped. "You know, you could have blocked your work calls."

He shook his head. "No, it needs to be a clean break. You and those sexy as hell shoes led me here and reminded me of the person I want to be in this world."

Shock and confusion marred her features. "You've known me for a day and a half, and I know it sounds crazy when I say this, but I'm cursed when it comes to love."

This damn Kiss Keeper Curse! He had to figure out a way around it.

"Natalie, you know I'm right about us. You know there's something more between us than two people pretending to be a couple."

"I know, but I've been wrong so many times," she said, focusing on the space between them.

"Six times isn't so many times," he pressed.

Pain flashed in her eyes. "Six broken hearts and all of them from Jakes. I'm starting to think that I'm not meant to have anyone. Maybe I'm supposed to be Jake-less."

No, she couldn't be right. There was a reason he'd ended up back here with her. They were meant to be together. But how the hell was he supposed to convince her when he couldn't reveal that he was her kiss keeper?

He glanced over at the shore and saw the outline of the old abandoned lighthouse. The abandoned lighthouse that wasn't far off from the Kiss Keeper's well. An idea sparked, and he grabbed the oars and started rowing.

Natalie gripped the sides of the boat. "Where are you going?"

"To break a curse," he answered, slicing the oars through the dark water.

She stared down at her feet. "I don't think it can be broken, Jake."

He had to try.

He rowed into a shallow, sleepy cove, and the boat grazed the ocean floor. Without waiting to hit dry land, he jumped out and pulled the boat onto the pebbly sand.

"That structure over there. It's the abandoned lighthouse, right?" he asked, playing stupid. He knew damn well where they were.

"Yes, this is the old Wiscasset lighthouse. How do you know about it?" she asked as he helped her out of the boat.

"Finn mentioned it when we were fishing today," he lied. "It's close to that well, right? The Kiss Keeper's well?"

"It's not too far," she answered, watching him closely.

"Tell me more about this curse," he said, taking her hand and leading her toward the lighthouse's crumbling outbuildings.

"The whole Kiss Keeper tale started with a young man who lived here and the kiss he never got to have with the young woman he loved."

They passed the lighthouse tower, and he ran his hand over a battered railing.

"Does anyone know what really happened to them?"

She released a heavy sigh. "I don't think so. Nobody knows what's fact or fiction anymore. All I ever heard was that the Wiscasset family used to mind this lighthouse. Otis Wiscasset was a young man who was supposed to take over the lighthouse after his father, but he'd fallen in love with a girl named Muriel Boothe. But Muriel's family was quite well-to-do, and they didn't want their daughter to marry a lowly lighthouse keeper. To make matters worse, her parents decided to send her back to England, that's where they were from, to try to stop the budding romance. But it was too late. She and Otis Wiscasset were already in love. The legend has it that the night before she was supposed to be shipped off, they'd agreed to meet at this well to have their first kiss. But it's said that Muriel never showed up, and Otis disappeared, never to be seen again."

That's how he remembered it, too.

"Curses have to have a way to be broken. I think it's a rule or something," he said, imagining Otis Wiscasset's pain when he realized the woman he loved was gone. Christ! What would he do if this didn't work?

"Which way to the well?" he asked, anticipation building in his chest.

Yes, he knew the answer, but needed to maintain the ruse.

"That trail will lead us there," she answered as they headed into the woods.

The thick coastal canopy of trees diffused the last rays of light. Shadows played off the foliage, but neither of them slowed. It was as if the well were calling to them, beckoning them back to the place where they first met fifteen years ago as strangers and left as cursed kiss keepers.

They passed a thicket of blackberries, and the sweet scent transported him back in time. Back to that night when he stumbled, blindfolded down the path that led from the teen boys' cabin to the old well.

"Jake," she whispered. "We're here."

It seemed crazy that they'd visited the well just this morning—like a thousand years had passed instead of less than a dozen hours. Hal was right. The hours did feel more like months here.

He led her to the stone structure, then took both her hands into his. "What if I kissed you here?"

She stared into the dark well. "The legend says that it has to be a first kiss offered up."

The heaviness in his chest made way for a lightness that centered him and slowed the hammering beat of his heart.

"What about a last kiss?"

She released his hands and took a clumsy step backward. "Holy crap! You *are* a part-time serial killer."

He gathered her into his arms. "I don't mean your last kiss ever. I mean that I want to be the last Jake you kiss."

"That still sounds pretty serial killer-ish," she answered, eyeing him closely, but she didn't pull away.

He tucked a lock of hair behind her ear. "How about this, I want to kiss you and then keep on kissing you."

She looked away. "I'm not just some girl that you swooped in and rescued from her family's ridicule. I have real responsibilities now. I can't fail, Jake. Too much is riding on this for me."

He rested his hand on her shoulder and brushed her collarbone with his thumb. "I understand, Heels, and I want to help you."

"*You* want to help *me* with Camp Woolwich?" she asked with a skeptical twist to her words.

He had to break through this barrier she'd erected.

"I want to be with you. If that means Camp Woolwich, then so be it. I want you, Natalie."

She stared down at his hand, resting on her shoulder. "What about your real life back in Denver?"

He slid his hand up to tilt her chin, then held her gaze in the misty darkness. "Nothing in the past fifteen years has been more real than the last two days I've spent with you."

"Wow, that sounds a lot less serial killer-ish," she said as wonder edged out the thread of disbelief in her voice.

Her walls were coming down. Could this place really be enchanted, or was the connection between them too strong to ignore? One or the other, that didn't change what he knew in his heart.

"Let me kiss you, Natalie. Let me kiss you, and let's put any talk of a curse behind us," he whispered into the air like a prayer.

The hint of a smile pulled at the corners of her mouth. "You want to be my seventh Jake?"

He shook his head. "No. I want to be the Jake who makes love to you every night and wakes up with you in my arms each morning."

She released a shaky breath. "That also definitely doesn't sound like a serial killer thing to say."

He closed the distance as his lips nearly grazed hers when she startled.

"What is it?" he asked, looking around for...ghosts or whatever creepy things hung out around old wells.

"We should do this right," she said, then tore two strips of fabric from her lobster bake luau skirt.

"You want me to blindfold you?" he asked.

"And then put one on yourself. That's how the kiss keeper works. The guy and the girl are supposed to be blindfolded. If we're going to try to break this curse, we might as well do everything," she replied, handing him the strips.

She had a point.

He took the fabric and pressed it over her eyes. "Is that okay? It's not too tight?" he asked, gently tying the blindfold.

She pressed her fingertips along the edge of the frayed material. "It's perfect. Now, it's your turn."

He stared down at her just as he had when he'd removed his blindfold all those years ago when the night patrol threw a wrench into their first kiss.

"Jake, are you ready?" she asked.

"Hold on," he said, securing his makeshift blindfold.

They stood there, frozen in time. It was like being thirteen again, except now, there was a lot more riding on this kiss.

"Hey, Heels?" he said, resting his hand on her hip.

"Yes."

He wanted to tell her everything. In the inky blackness, while wearing a blindfold decked with tiny lobsters, he wanted a clean slate. He wanted to erase the past fifteen years and confess, but her voice halted that train of thought.

She pressed her hands to his chest and twisted the fabric of his shirt. "Jake?"

"Yeah?"

"Kiss me," she whispered.

In the space of a breath, he forgot his past. He forgot the heartache of losing his parents and the emptiness of a career spent wheeling and dealing and amassing a fortune that never felt like enough. Here, in this place, he was solely Natalie Callahan's kiss keeper. He pulled her in close and pressed a whisper-soft kiss to the corner of her mouth.

She hummed a contented sigh as the sound of the hypnotic ebb and flow of the ocean carried in on the night breeze. At Camp Woolwich, a million miles from where he thought he'd end up, holding the girl he could never forget, he was home.

"Natalie, I..." he began, not even knowing where to start when she pressed her index finger to his lips and silenced him.

"I think we need to go big time on this kissing business,"

she said with a smile in her voice as she wrapped her arms around his neck.

"You want big time?" he asked, lowering his voice.

"Curse busting big time," she challenged.

He gripped her ass, lifted her into his arms, and held her flush against his body. "Challenge accepted," he answered, then captured her mouth in the exact opposite of anything that could be described as whisper-soft.

The friction between their bodies ignited an explosive kiss. Her fingers tangled in the hair at the nape of his neck as she rocked against him. Lips and tongues met in a primal dance as their inhibitions disintegrated into the darkness. Without the gift of sight, his other senses heightened as he grew hard, wanting to devour every inch of the woman in his arms.

He pressed her back to one of the stone pillars that supported the well's worn wooden roof, then kissed a trail to her earlobe. "You taste like blackberries and sweet cream," he said, his voice a low gravelly rumble.

She bucked her hips, grinding into him as her smooth skin and soft curves sent his pulse racing. He thrust his hips in rhythm with her and pressed his hard length against her in the hottest session of dry-humping he was positive this well had ever seen.

Natalie's soft sighs fed his desire, but he hungered for more. More of her scent. More of her touch. He ran his tongue along the shell of her ear, tasting her, and she moaned his name.

"*Jake.*"

The syllable hung hot and heavy in the air, dripping with a deep yearning that echoed his ravenousness, unbridled drive to toss aside that damn skirt, tear off her panties, and thrust his cock into her sweet heat.

"I want to feel you. I want all of you," he rasped.

"Then, take me. I'm yours," she said, gasping as he continued to piston his hips.

He stilled and pressed his forehead to hers. "You are?"

She ran her fingertips along his jawline. "I think I was a goner from the moment you threw me over your shoulder to make our flight. That feels like a lifetime ago, doesn't it?"

But she had him before that.

The image of her, standing across from him after they made it through security, flashed in his mind. The world had blurred around them, binding them together as if their fate had already been sealed, their destinies merging right there a few steps away from the TSA screening line where their lives had intersected for a second time.

His breaths grew ragged. Of course, he wanted her, but he didn't want this moment to end with a quick and dirty screw against a stone pillar. Carefully, he set her down, then kneeled in front of her.

"What are you doing?" she asked as he slid his hands down her torso.

"How much do you like this skirt?" he asked, twisting a string of fabric.

"Even less than my panties," she answered, playfully twisting a lock of his hair.

"Good answer," he replied.

Natalie gasped as he slowly removed the luau costume, then slid her panties down her slim legs. Gripping her ass in both hands, he kissed a line from her hip down to the apex of her thighs, then hooked her left leg over his shoulder and tasted her sweet center.

"You've risen to the challenge," she moaned as he worked her into a frenzy.

Her body trembled with the promise of release. Her

gasps and tight breaths sent a heated charge through his veins. And then she was there, balancing on the edge of sweet release. Twisting her fingers in his hair, she succumbed to her desire.

"Jake, oh, yes!" she panted, winding down.

But they weren't done yet—not even close. If this was their chance to break the Kiss Keeper Curse, he was not about to half-ass it.

Prowling the length of her body, he kissed his way up, pausing to give special attention to the delicate skin below her earlobe. Natalie hummed her gratification, and the sound went straight to his hard length. With her taste on his tongue, their mouths met in a fury of feverish passion. He needed to have her right there. Curse or no curse, she was his.

With her chest heaving, Natalie broke their kiss then turned in his arms. Her ass brushed against his hard length, and he was done holding back. Unclasping his pants, he shrugged out of them. When he reached for her, his hands met her hips. She'd hinged forward, presenting her perfect ass.

He caressed the soft flesh. "You're beautiful."

Positioning himself at her entrance, he drove into her wet heat. One hand on her hip and the other reaching around to caress her tight bundle of nerves, he took her from behind in slow, deliberate strokes, savoring each delicious thrust. But the urge to let loose and allow his lust to take over prevailed. Their bodies met in a punishing rhythm that quickly had them gasping, balancing on the tightrope between two worlds—one where they were two bodies and the other where their souls became one.

She cried out, tightening around him. He tore off his blindfold and then hers. He had to see her, had to look into her eyes when they met their release. She arched her back and turned her head. His fingertips pressed into the soft flesh of her hips as their eyes met in the darkness. He let go, spilling into her, shedding the past and promising himself he'd be the kind of man who deserved a future with her. Pistoning his hips and working her sensitive bud, they journeyed into oblivion together, their bodies writhing as they rode out wave after wave of pleasure.

He pulled out and gathered Natalie into his arms. She rested her head in the crook of his neck. She was warm, so warm in his arms as she melted into his embrace.

"Do you think it worked?" she asked, her breath tickling his neck.

Did they break the curse or was what he'd held back—the truth of his connection to her and this place—still a threat?

He tightened his hold on her. He'd make it work. He had to. He'd figure out a way to get Charlie off the scent and keep Camp Woolwich intact.

He tilted her face up and pressed his lips to hers as a chill ran through him. "One more kiss, just to be sure," he said, praying that somewhere out there, the spirit of Otis Wiscasset would relinquish his hold and lift the Kiss Keeper Curse.

10

NATALIE

Natalie picked out a cowgirl hat and placed it on her head, then checked her reflection in the mirror and could hardly recognize the woman who couldn't seem to wipe the smile from her face.

Over the past three days, she and Jake had decided not to leave anything to chance when it came to the Kiss Keeper Curse. And, to be on the safe side, they agreed not to limit their kissing to just the well.

He'd kissed her in the boathouse, in the dining hall, in the art room, in the lodge, behind every cabin, in the garden, along the coast at sunset, along the coast at midday, and at the old crumbling Wiscasset lighthouse. He even kissed her in one of the camp's Sunfish sailboats. Granted, it was tied to a piling on the waterfront, and her real boyfriend —oh, how she loved the sound of that—had one foot in the boat while the other was firmly planted on the dock. But after learning what had happened to his parents, she knew it was a big step for him.

This new life was a big step for both of them.

The buttoned-up, stone-faced man with his phone

blowing up and every hair on his head perfectly in place had disappeared. In its place was her Jake. The Jake, true to his word that set her body on fire every night with his touch and held her close until morning.

"Tell me why I have to wear this get-up?" he asked, coming out of the dressing room and looking like cowboy sex on a stick in snug-fitting jeans, a plaid shirt, and a Stetson hat.

Her heart fluttered at the sight of him. "Did the bazillion tiny paper cowboy hats you hung from the rafters in the barn not clue you in?"

Tonight, her grandparents had planned a good old-fashioned barn dance with fiddles and square dancing to boot. While everyone had gone into town earlier to purchase western wear, she and Jake had offered to stay behind, haul out all the sports equipment stored inside the barn, and set up for the event. It only made sense. The camp was going to be their responsibility soon. A thought that a week ago would have terrified her. But with Jake by her side, it felt right. With her background as an educator and his business and real estate knowledge, everything seemed to be fitting into place.

He came to her side next to a display of belt buckles and looked her up and down.

"What?" she asked, checking her little denim skirt and red plaid cowgirl top.

"You better step into the dressing room so I can fix your shirt," he replied with a twist of a grin.

"What's wrong with it?" she asked, darting into the tight space. Had she missed a button? Was her bra showing?

She tied the tails of the shirt into a little bow in the front and thought she'd nailed barn dance casual.

"It's on," he said, his gaze darkening as he pressed her

back against the dressing room mirror and undid her top button.

"Slow down, cowboy. We have a barn full of people to get back to. And there's no way I'm missing out on dancing in these," she added, kicking up her heel to reveal a cowgirl boot.

He turned his attention to her footwear. "Do you remember how I said that your stilettos were my favorite?"

"Yes."

"Now, I have two favorites," he answered, then leaned in to kiss her when the brims of their hats bumped.

"That's a sign," she said with a chuckle.

"That you need to be wearing nothing but those boots?" he threw back.

She adjusted his hat. "No, that we need to get back to camp. We'll save the boots for later tonight."

"I like that plan," he replied with a wicked grin, then glanced down at his outfit. "Should I change back into my regular clothes?"

They'd driven into town, but they were a good twenty minutes away, and the barn dance was due to start in half an hour.

Natalie glanced at her watch. "No time. We should wear them back and head straight to the barn."

Jake paid for their outfits, and they stepped out onto the small town's Main Street, where they got a few odd looks.

"Not too many New England cowboys," he said, tipping his hat to an elderly couple who hurried past them.

She hooked her arm with his. "Luckily, the one western shop in the area isn't too far from us, and it is a Camp—"

"Woolwich tradition," he finished as they strolled back to the camp van.

"It's not such a stretch that the same place that hosts a

lobster bake luau could also put on a western barn dance night," she countered.

"We could add a pirate night when we take over. Who doesn't love a pirate? Or an alien night," Jake offered.

"An alien night?" she questioned.

He shrugged. "Yeah, everyone could dress up as little green men. We could get a laser machine and put on a show at the waterfront. It would be great!"

She tightened her hold on his arm. Her boyfriend's arm. Her partner's arm. She was about to embark on a life-changing endeavor, and she wasn't alone. She leaned into him, and he wrapped his arm around her. Her string of terrible Jakes had led her to the one good one out there.

"We'll see about the lasers," she said when a familiar voice called out from behind them.

"Look, it's Adam, the cowboy!"

They turned to see the retired sisters from the convent who'd come to the camp for the art lesson.

"It's lovely to see you. What brings you to town?" Natalie asked the women.

"Gin," Sister Evangeline, the sassy nun who had a thing for Jake, answered as she swallowed him up with her eyes.

"Gin! Wow, I didn't think nuns drank," Natalie replied.

The little nun shook her head. "Nobody bats an eyelash at a bunch of drunk monks brewing beer, but when a nun has a hankering for a nice gin martini, people think that the Savior himself should send a swarm of locusts to stop her."

"When we're in town, we sometimes enjoy an alcoholic beverage, in moderation, of course," Sister Anne said, then leaned in. "And it keeps Sister Evangeline from getting too cranky and too handsy with the gardener. Poor, Dominic," she said, then made the sign of the cross.

"I can feel Dominic's pain," Jake said under his breath as he blushed under Sister Evangeline's penetrating gaze.

"Will you be leaving Maine soon? The anniversary celebration is set to conclude in a couple of days, right?" Sister Anne asked.

Natalie grinned as a wave of excitement laced with trepidation coursed through her body.

"Actually, Jake and I are staying. We're going to be taking over the camp for my grandparents."

Sister Anne made the sign of the cross again. "I'm so glad to hear that. It would have been a shame if they'd had to close. Your grandparents do so much for this community."

Natalie shared a look with Jake. "Why would you say that?"

Sister Anne's features grew pensive. "We were very worried and kept your grandparents in our prayers. It was touch and go about a year ago."

"What was touch and go?" she asked, completely in the dark.

Sister Anne cocked her head to the side. "When your grandfather had pneumonia."

Pneumonia? This was the first she'd heard of that. But that could explain his thinner frame and lingering cough.

"I didn't know that my grandfather had been sick."

The nun patted her arm. "He was quite ill. I believe he spent a week in the hospital. I visited him and your grandmother a few times."

"I don't understand why they didn't tell me or anyone in the family," Natalie replied.

The nun smiled sympathetically. "I don't think your grandparents wanted to burden any of you, dear. They got through it, and your grandfather seems to be doing much better now. It must be such a relief for them to know that they'll have some time to relax and enjoy life. They work so hard."

Natalie's mind was reeling when Sister Evangeline piped up.

"I'd like some time to relax, too! We just finished volunteering at the library, in the children's area of all places. The polar opposite of relaxing!"

"How about we go in and have that drink," Sister Anne suggested, biting back a grin as the women entered the tavern.

Natalie shook her head. "What do you make of that, Jake?"

"Six nuns walk into a tavern? It sounds like the beginning of a pretty bad joke," he offered, but she wasn't in the mood to laugh.

"No, my grandfather's illness, and how they didn't tell anyone in the family."

He took her hand and threaded their fingers together as they continued down the sidewalk. "Not everyone is an open book, Natalie."

"Yes, but if my grandfather was sick, I could have done something to help."

He squeezed her hand. "You are doing something to help. You're taking over the camp. They're lucky they have you."

She glanced up at him. "You mean us. They're lucky to have us."

He smiled, but it didn't quite reach his eyes. "Yeah, that's what I meant. But, Natalie, your grandparents are getting older. There are probably things they'd like to do while they can. Maybe this bout of pneumonia made them realize that."

Jake opened the passenger side door to the old camp van and helped her in, then settled himself in the driver's seat.

She took off her cowgirl hat and set it on her lap. "I can't believe I missed the signs. There was a time about a year ago when I couldn't get ahold of them. I figured that they were busy with summer camp preparations. But it wasn't that at all. It's so hard to believe. My grandparents always seemed larger than life to me. It's hard to think of them as..."

"Just people?" Jake offered.

"Yes, and the notion that the camp might have become too much for them," she added.

He started the van and merged into traffic. "It's good that they have options."

She stared at his profile. "What do you mean, options?"

"Well, if you and I weren't taking over, they could always sell. Your grandpa did mention that he was considering it."

Heat coursed through her veins. "Yes, maybe for a second, but I don't think he'd do it. This place is too important."

"Natalie, don't get angry. I'm only saying that there are always options—especially when you have to take into account someone's health," Jake replied gently.

She nodded and forced herself to take a breath. Jake bought and sold property for a living. It made sense that he'd take that possibility into consideration, but that didn't mean it didn't shake her to the core.

"I'm not going to let anything happen to Camp Wool-wich," she said.

The responsibility already weighed on her, but now the true magnitude of what she—and Jake—had volunteered to do hit home, and it hit home hard. If she failed, her grand-parents most likely wouldn't be able to swoop in and help.

"We won't let it fail. You're not doing this alone. You've

got me," he said, lifting her hand and pressing a kiss to her palm. "And you could probably get Leo on board to do just about anything you needed if you showed him your feet every so often."

She shook her head and chuckled. "You're probably right, but ew."

"Look at that! A Jake ranks higher than a podiatrist," he teased.

She sat back and drank in his beautiful face. "You're not just *a* Jake. You're my Jake."

He glanced at his watch. "A Jake who needs to hit the gas if we don't want to be late."

She stared out the window as they traveled the familiar roads. "And don't forget, you need to take the next turn— which you'd know if you had a phone with GPS. The Maine roads can be tricky." She still couldn't believe he'd thrown his cell into the ocean. She turned her attention back to him. "Are you sure you don't want to get a new phone? We could always head into Portland tomorrow and pick up another."

A muscle twitched in his cheek. "I'm not ready to deal with that world yet."

"You'll have to eventually, though, right?" she asked. He'd been reticent about his work, but he was technically on vacation. Still, the way his phone had pinged and chimed before he'd sent it to a watery grave made her think he'd had quite a bit going on.

"I'm still working a few things out in my head, Heels." He reached over and squeezed her knee. "It'll be fine."

It wasn't long before they exited the main road and headed down the camp's bumpy drive. Jake pulled into the makeshift parking area. The gravel lot was empty when they'd left, but now several cars squeezed into the small space.

"Who else is coming?" he asked, scanning the nearly full lot as he helped her out.

She put on her cowgirl hat, then noticed a swank BMW tucked between a few older model sedans.

"The cars probably belong to the musicians. I thought tonight was going to be just friends and family, but knowing my grandparents, they could have invited some community group."

"At least we know Sister Evangeline is back in that tavern with her gin. God only knows what she'd do to me at a barn dance," Jake said with an exaggerated cringe.

"I imagine your do-si-do dance card would be filled all night," she said, then she gasped.

"What? Did you remember that the nuns were invited?" he asked as real panic flashed in his eyes.

She shook her head. "No, the nuns aren't coming. At least, I don't think they are. But we need to hurry. I just remembered that as the lobster luau queen, it's my duty to kick off the barn dance."

"Lucky for you, I'm wearing barn dancing shoes," he replied, admiring his new boots.

She tossed him a wink. "You might not get the first dance, cowboy."

He took her hand as they set off on the trail that led to the camp's old barn. "Why not?"

"The way it works is that everyone puts their name in a hat, and the lobster queen has the first dance with the lucky winner."

He pursed his lips and seemed to weigh the answer. "What if I write my name on all the slips of paper?"

"Then you'd be a cheater," she said, meeting his devious gaze.

"A cheater who plays to win," he replied, eyes twinkling.

"It's one dance, Jake."

"What if I don't want to share?" he offered as his voice took on a low, rumbling edge.

"Do you always get what you want?" she asked as heat flooded her body, secretly loving how this man didn't want to share her for even one dance.

"I'm here with you, aren't I?" he tossed back with a cocky grin that said he did get what he wanted.

She parted her lips, hoping a pithy comeback would materialize, but lost her train of thought as they rounded the bend to find the barn transformed. In the twilight, the twinkling lights they'd spent hours hanging lit the space in a cozy glow while the wildflowers she'd picked with the children earlier in the day were displayed in mason jars on top of blue checkered tablecloths that dotted the space around the dance floor. The once dreary and dank barn now sparkled with country charm as a fiddler tuned his instrument, setting the perfect soundscape.

"It's..." she said, searching for the right word as adults laughed and chatted under a canopy of light while children weaved their way past the grownups to a table lined with sweet treats and pitchers of lemonade.

"You're right. It's..." Jake began when a clap of thunder and a smattering of raindrops darkened the gravel path.

"Oh, no! Our barn dance," she cried.

He wrapped his arm around her and ushered her inside. "I was up on that roof all afternoon, hanging lights and those little hats of yours. The structure is sound. We should be fine."

"The lobster queen has arrived," her grandmother said,

greeting them each with a hug. "And just in the nick of time. It looks like we're in for some rain."

Her grandfather joined them. "Come on in and see how wonderfully the barn turned out. You kids did a great job," he said with a healthy grin, but Natalie couldn't forget what the nuns had shared and wrapped her arms around the man.

Her grandfather patted her back. "What's all this, Nat?"

"I'm just glad to be here," she answered, blinking back tears.

"Get used to it, kiddo. You're taking over," he said with a sly-dog smile.

"And this time next week, your grandfather and I will be boarding a plane and heading to Maui for a real Hawaiian luau. We've never had a summer to ourselves," her grandmother answered with a girlish blush.

Natalie shared a glance with Jake. "That's wonderful news! You deserve many, many more summers together."

"Well, it certainly gives us great peace of mind to know the camp will be in good hands," her grandma Bev added as Finn joined them, holding a cowboy hat brimming with folded pieces of paper.

"Uncle Jake, do you want to put your name in the hat for a chance to dance with Aunt Nat?"

"Absolutely," he answered as Finn's expression grew serious.

"But you only get one piece of paper. I caught Uncle Leo trying to sneak in two!" the boy replied.

"I'm not surprised," Jake said, tossing her a knowing look. "Who wouldn't want to dance with your Aunt Natalie? She's the prettiest lobster queen I've ever seen."

Finn frowned then turned to her. "I guess you're not that bad for a girl, Aunt Nat, and you're good at climbing trees."

"That's what I like about her, too," Jake said, clapping Finn on the shoulder.

The adults chuckled as Jake took the offered marker and slip of paper and entered to win the first dance.

Finn scanned the room, then held up the hat. "Okay, everybody! This is your last chance to enter to win the first dance with the lobster queen," the boy cried as the room quieted.

"I'd like to enter," offered an unfamiliar voice.

Natalie glanced over her shoulder at the stranger. "I'm sorry, I don't think we've met."

"No, we haven't. I work with Jake Teller," the man replied with a smug grin as the room grew silent, and all eyes fell on them.

"Charlie? My goodness, is that you? What are you doing here?" her grandmother asked, looking at the man as if she'd seen a ghost.

Natalie touched Jake's arm. "Who is this?"

Jake stiffened. "This is Charlie Linton, my boss."

"Your boss? Why would your boss come here?" She'd had a feeling that something was up with Jake's work, but to have his boss track him down on vacation seemed absurd. And even crazier, why would her grandmother know this man?

"I'm here because Jake seems to have lost his way and forgot who was still in charge," this Charlie replied with a cold bend to his words.

"In charge of what?" she asked, getting sick and tired of not knowing what the hell was going on.

Jake took her hand. "I've held something back from you, Natalie. Something I should have told you. I just didn't know how."

She glanced from Jake to his boss. "Tell me what's going on?"

"For starters, this isn't Jake's first visit to Camp Woolwich, is it, son?" her grandfather said.

This was getting to be too much. She released Jake's hand and took a step back. "What are you talking about, Grandpa?"

Her grandfather's gaze softened. "The first night when your grandmother thought she recognized Jake, it was because he'd been here before—as a camper."

Natalie inhaled a tight breath. "A camper? When?"

"When I was thirteen," Jake answered, his gaze trained on the barn floor.

The room went topsy-turvy. Or maybe it was just her mind spinning. "Why didn't you tell me, Jake, and Grandpa, if you knew, why didn't you say something?"

"Because once your grandfather and I figured out who Jake was, we knew that coming back here had to be hard for him. We wanted to give him some time," her grandmother offered.

"Time for what?" Nat asked, trying to make sense of it all.

"Jake's parents didn't pick him up from camp after the summer ended because they'd passed away," her grandmother answered, and the penny dropped.

"Your parents died in a boating accident while you were here at Camp Woolwich?" she said, the words tumbling out.

He met her gaze with his eyes clouded with pain and nodded.

"We'd always wondered what happened to you, dear," her grandmother offered gently.

"You've known who I was from that first night?" he asked, lifting his chin a fraction.

Hal nodded. "Yes, after you all left, Bev and I looked at the camp picture, then checked our records and found a Jacob Teller on the camper log. My wife never forgets a face."

Natalie's jaw dropped, but before she was able to get a word in, Charlie Linton cleared his throat.

"I hate to break up this touching moment, but Jake's not here because he wanted to have a heart to heart Kumbaya moment with you people. He's here because I sent him to get *my* land back." The man eyed Jake. "Except, it looks like my protégé is trying to keep it all for himself and cut me out of the deal."

Jake shook his head as his gaze turned cold. "That's not true."

Charlie crossed his arms. "What was your plan? Use the girl to get the land then convince her to sell it to you? If I didn't think you were trying to screw me out of a deal, I'd say it was a genius idea."

"You wanted to try to get my family to sell Camp Wool-wich?" she said, glaring at Jake, the man she thought she might...no, she couldn't go there.

"Where'd you even get the idea Camp Woolwich was for sale? You've left us alone for fifty years. What made you think you could get it now?" her grandfather said, his cheeks growing pink with anger.

Charlie turned away, and Hal scoffed.

"Don't tell me we're playing this game. Look me in the eye like a man, Linton."

"You're no man. You're the scoundrel who took my land," Charlie bit back.

Hal chuckled, a dry, sarcastic little sound. "Look at Mr. Sour Grapes over here. It's been fifty years, and you're still stewing, and you and I both know that I won this land fair and square."

Charlie's eyes flashed with anger. "That may be true, but you stole Bev away from me. We were friends, Hal, and you knew how I felt about her."

Natalie watched, wide-eyed, as this love triangle unfolded.

Her grandmother's features softened. "I was never yours like that, Charlie. We were always friends, dear friends."

"Until this card shark swooped into our lives and ruined everything for me," he shot back like a sullen teenager.

"You know that's not how it happened," Bev said gently.

"And you're the one who racked up all those gambling debts, Charlie. Not me. If you remember right, I tried to get you to go home and cut your losses," Hal answered.

A sour look marred Charlie's expression. "I don't need advice from you, Hal Woolwich. I've made a fortune over the last fifty years in real estate, and losing this piece of land, land that had been in my family for generations, was the only mistake I've ever made, and I'm not about to let it go unchecked. I know you're thinking of selling. Name your price."

"Wherever did you get the idea we'd want to sell to you?" Bev asked.

"Oh, that would be me."

Everyone's gaze bounced to...Lara?

"You?" Leslie exclaimed, staring at her sister.

Lara twisted a strand of hair around her finger like a six-year-old. "Yeah, remember when Gram called and wanted to talk to you about Grandpa last year when he got sick?"

Leslie stared at her sister. "You heard that call?"

"Oh yeah, Les! I can hear everything you do from my office," the bubblehead answered.

"I didn't think we were going to tell the kids," Hal said, turning to his wife.

"I called Leslie because she's a doctor. You didn't want to go into the hospital, and I needed her reassurance that it was the right thing to do," her grandmother said as the family murmured in the background.

Hal raised his hands to quiet them down. "Here it is, everyone. I had pneumonia last year, and your grandmother and I didn't want to trouble anyone. As you can see, I'm doing much better."

"What about the cough?" Natalie asked as the pieces started coming together.

"It's taking me a while to get back to one hundred percent. I pick up a cold here and there much easier these days," her grandfather answered.

"What I don't understand, Lara, dear, is why you would tell Charlie Linton about Grandpa? How would you even know to contact him?" her grandmother asked.

"Cinnamon rolls and money," Lara answered as if that could explain everything.

"Help us understand, dear," Bev pressed.

Lara nodded. "Sure! I thought that with Grandpa's deteriorating health, you might consider selling the camp if the right offer came your way. Right now, the Woolwich trust lays out that the profits of a sale would be split between the family, and Marcus and I needed the money to save our podiatric practice."

Leslie went white. "You took the money? Leo and I have been going out of our minds, trying to figure out what happened. We thought it was an accounting error."

"Oh, no!" Marcus chimed in. "That's where the cinnamon rolls come in. Lara and I wanted to surprise you and Leo, so we invested the majority of the practice's capital in foot inserts that smell like cinnamon rolls. But it turns out that nobody wants their feet to smell like pastry. We lost a ton of money."

Leslie's jaw dropped as Leo came to her side and took her hand.

"But, Lara, that doesn't answer how you found Charlie?" her grandmother nudged.

The woman smiled like a game show hostess. "Oh, that's easy! We all know that grandpa won this land in a card game. I figured whoever lost it may still be mad about it. Losing a huge chunk of land in a card game would be a very foolish thing to do."

"Like investing in cinnamon-scented shoe inserts?" Leslie said under her breath as Leo patted her back.

Lara nodded, undeterred. "Yeah, exactly! So, I searched the land records and traced the land back to the Wiscasset family. Well, there aren't any Wiscassets around here anymore, so I did a search of women with the maiden name and then searched for their married names, and that's how I found Mr. Linton, the real estate mogul. It was tricky. The Wiscasset family name disappeared after a few generations with the birth of all daughters, but I had a feeling a Wiscasset relative with a huge real estate business would be a good place to start."

Leslie shook her head. "You're smart enough to figure all that out but not able to grasp that cinnamon roll-scented shoe inserts would be a terrible idea?"

"We all have our gifts, Les. Oh! Look, Marcus! There are oatmeal raisin cookies on the dessert table," Lara answered as her gnat-like attention span took over, and she and Marcus made a beeline for the treats.

The room remained still as Lara and Marcus raided the desserts.

"You're a Wiscasset? I thought you grew up in Boston," Jake said.

Charlie looked away. "My great-great-grandmother married a Wiscasset, and this land was passed down to me."

Her grandmother stepped forward and touched Charlie's arm. "And then you lost it, Charlie, and Hal and I built a life here. I'm sorry that you're so bitter. If you'd only come to us, you know we would have welcomed you with open arms."

The man's expression softened as he met her grandmother's gaze, but in the blink of an eye, his hardened disposition returned, and he glared at Jake.

"Mark my words, kid. You're done in this business," the man said, then strode out into the rain.

Natalie caught her breath and stared up at Jake.

"Natalie, I—"

"Hold on a minute," Leslie interrupted with a beady gaze. "How do we know that Natalie's not a part of this? What if that guy was right, and she and her boyfriend had planned to try to get this land and then sell it or develop it themselves? If you and Grandpa and Grandma signed everything over to Natalie, she could alter the family trust and take everything."

Heat rose to Natalie's cheeks. "I would never do that?"

"You were the one who brought Jake here. He's your boyfriend," Leslie challenged.

Shame flooded her system. She wasn't the only one who'd been dishonest. Natalie glanced at Jake and knew what she had to do.

"Jake's not my boyfriend."

"Natalie, wait," he said, but she raised her hand to stop him.

She steadied herself. "Here's the truth. I met Jake at the

airport on the way to Maine. I'd just gotten dumped by my boyfriend, Jake, and then I met this Jake, Jake Teller, in the security line. We became acquainted and then found ourselves on the same flight. When we got off the plane and saw Leslie and Lara at the airport, I asked, well, begged him to spend the week with me and pretend to be my boyfriend."

"Oh my, God!" Leslie sneered as the events of Jake agreeing to her proposal took on a new light.

She turned to her fake or real or God, she didn't know anymore, boyfriend as an awareness washed over her like a punch to the gut. "You only agreed to come after Fish met us at the baggage claim, and you learned that I was part of the Woolwich family. I thought you did it because you liked me."

She was an idiot. A complete idiot for falling for this con man.

"I do like you, Natalie," he pleaded.

She shook her head as the sickening sensation remained. "No, you only liked what I could do for you. You used me."

"It's not like that anymore," he whispered.

"But that's how it started, right? Otherwise, you would have told me that you knew of Camp Woolwich and that you'd come here as a boy. You don't want me. You want this land. You're no different than your boss."

"There's more," he said in a pained breath.

She threw up her hands. "What more could there be?"

He held her gaze. "Remember that night when you were thirteen and went to the Kiss Keeper's well?"

"What about it?"

He swallowed hard. "It was me, at the well. I was the boy. I'm your kiss keeper."

She shook her head. "No, no, you can't be him. You're lying."

"I'm not."

"How can I believe you?" she whispered, sounding as if the wind had been knocked out of her.

He closed the distance between them and set his hand on her shoulder, then brushed his thumb across her collarbone, and she gasped, remembering when he'd done the same thing fifteen years ago.

"Because, before I left you and ran back to my cabin, I told you that kissing you was better than sailing across the lake."

The breath caught in Natalie's throat, and she was that blindfolded girl, again—her heart beating like a drum just as it had after she'd had her first kiss. She'd never told a soul about what her kiss keeper had said to her before he disappeared into the night. It hadn't made much sense at the time, and she'd been reeling from not only the most perfect first kiss but from evading the night patrol.

"It's you," she said on a tight whisper.

A flash of hope shined in his eyes. "I'm sorry. I screwed up. I never wanted to hurt you, Natalie. I—"

She stepped back, and the tangle of humiliation, shame, and astonishment inside her went numb as one truth made itself known loud and clear.

The Kiss Keeper Curse hadn't been broken.

She pushed past him and ran out into the rain.

"Natalie, please, stop! We need to talk. I never wanted it to be like this," he called, coming after her, but she had to get away from him.

Her cowgirl hat flew off as she sprinted toward the waterfront with Jake close on her heels.

Heels.

Tears ran down her cheeks, mingling with the rain. She should have known this would happen. She should have been smarter than to trust a man she'd know for less than a week. And more than that, she should have remembered the curse.

Her boots clapped against the worn wooden dock as she snagged a lifejacket from a hook and spied her escape. Strapping on the jacket, she stepped into the small Sunfish sailboat and slid in the centerboard.

"Natalie, what are you doing?"

"Not flying," she bit out as she rigged the small two-person boat, preparing to sail.

"It's raining," he said, his voice shaking.

"I'm going to Woolwich Island. I need to be alone," she said, securing the mask and pulling up the sail.

With his toes edged up to the end of the dock, he ran his hands down his face. "I'm sorry, so damn sorry, Heels. Don't go!"

Her heart shattered, but she waved off his words. "Don't apologize. It's easier this way."

"Why would it be easier?" he asked, anguish lacing his words.

She untied the boat from the rusty cleat, freeing it from the dock, then pushed off as inches of water between them became feet then yards.

She swallowed back a sob. "Because now, all you are is just another Jake who broke my heart."

11

Natalie drew the brush across the canvas. Stroke after stroke, she blended the blues and greens until an angry churning sea engulfed the white backdrop, swallowing up a tiny battered rowboat. After all the revelations, and after all the deception came to light, she'd gone where Jake couldn't follow her—the ocean.

Perhaps, it was cruel, setting off into the same sea where he'd lost his parents, but she'd had no choice. And it wasn't like she'd gone far. She'd sailed the short distance to Woolwich Island, hundreds of times. Despite the rain, the winds had been relatively calm, and she'd reached her refuge with no problems. And that's where she'd stayed until the sun rose and then she'd sailed back to camp in the first threads of dawn. She hadn't gone back to the cottage she'd shared with Jake. She couldn't risk seeing him or worse than that, remembering what they'd shared. Instead, she'd holed up in the arts and crafts room, sustaining herself on packets of trail mix and soda from the vending machine in the lodge.

And that's where she'd spent another day and night, painting. She'd poured herself onto the canvas. With powerful strokes and broken, jagged lines, she laid out her soul in the shades of the ocean as a newfound peace set in.

Maybe she'd been the screw-up Woolwich granddaughter, but staring across the cove after a night on Woolwich Island and watching the veil of darkness rise to reveal the camp that she'd loved her whole life, she knew she belonged here. The curse may have cost her the love of a partner, but she wasn't about to let it hinder the connection she had to this place.

And, despite her broken heart that still longed for Jake's touch, that had to be enough.

If her grandparents still wanted her, she was ready to dedicate her life to Camp Woolwich.

She wiped a lock of hair from her forehead with the back of her hand and concentrated on the composition coming together in front of her when a knock at the door pulled her attention from the painting.

"Natalie, can we come in?" her grandmother called from the hallway.

"Sure," she answered, then set down her palette, rested the brush on a sheet of old newspaper, and stared at her latest painting.

"There's more depth to your work now," her grandma said, coming to her side.

"It's not the silly blackberry bush nature scene I used to paint over and over again," she replied, thinking back to when she and her grandmother would come here and paint. Artist in Residence, Beverly Woolwich, working on a masterpiece for a show, and little Natalie Callahan, content with her berries and butterflies.

Grandma Bev crossed her arms, taking in the watery landscape. "Those were good, too. But when I look at this, I see wisdom."

Natalie laughed, a tired, ragged sound. "After everything that's happened, I'm not sure I can boast that quality."

"Well, I see green and blue," her Grandpa Hal said, cocking his head to the side. "Oh, and there's a boat," he added as she shared a look with her grandmother, who pressed her lips together, suppressing a chuckle.

Her grandpa glanced around the room, then gestured to a trio of stools. "Can we sit and have a chat?"

Natalie wiped her hands on an old rag, ignoring the paint crusted to her nail beds, and joined her grandparents. Everyone had left her alone these last couple of days. She hadn't changed her clothes or left the lodge and probably looked like a zombie cowgirl by this point, but she knew that, eventually, her grandparents would come to find her. She could only hope that it wasn't to tell her that they didn't trust her with the camp.

"We owe you an apology, Natalie," her grandfather said, folding his hands on the oak table dusted with a smattering of dried paint.

Nat shook her head. "I think you've got that turned around. I'm the one who owes you both an apology. I'm the one who brought a fake boyfriend here that happened to want to steal the camp out from under our family. But I've had some time to think, and I know that beyond a doubt, my place is here. I hope that you'll still allow me to take over Camp Woolwich." She steadied herself. "And I can promise you one more thing. I'm done trying to find Mr. Right. You don't have to worry about me parading a bunch of strangers here ever again."

"Of course, we don't have to worry. You've already found your Mr. Right," her grandma answered with a quizzical look.

"Jake?" she sputtered as her grandparents nodded.

Natalie threw up her hands. "How, after everything that he kept from me, could I trust him with the camp?"

And her heart. But she wasn't about to go there with her grandparents.

"Because you love him, kiddo," her grandpa Hal replied with a New Englander no-nonsense shrug.

Nat's jaw dropped. "Love him? Grandpa, I met him at the airport a week ago. Who falls in love that fast?"

Her grandparents shared a knowing look.

"Everyone gets so wrapped up in the story about your grandfather winning this land in a hand of poker and how we got married here the next day that most don't even ask us how or even when we met," her grandmother said with a twinkle in her eyes.

Natalie reared back. "You're right. I figured you guys were together before he won the land. So, I'll bite, when did you meet?"

Her grandfather took her grandmother's hand. "The day before we got married."

"The day. As in, you knew each other for twenty-four hours before you decided to take vows to be together forever?" Natalie shot back.

Bev tapped her chin. "Well, it was more like thirty-two hours. I met your grandfather around lunchtime on a Friday, and I married him a little after dinner on Saturday."

"How could you know so fast?" Natalie asked.

"Sometimes, you just know," her grandmother answered.

Nat leaned forward. "How did your whirlwind romance even start?"

"It was fifty years ago, and it feels like yesterday," Hal began. "You see, Natalie, Charlie Linton was a friend of mine from college. He was quite impulsive back then and had gotten himself into some trouble playing cards. He owed the wrong people a good amount of money. When he told me that he was going back home to pick up some cash he had stashed in his childhood room and then planned on playing in a high-stakes poker game that night, I told him I wanted to tag along. But I was really there to try to keep him out of trouble."

"And I grew up next door to Charlie. We'd been friends for years, and he introduced me to your grandfather," her Grandma Bev added.

Natalie glanced between her grandparents. "And it was love at first sight?"

Her grandmother chuckled. "Oh, heavens, no! I thought your grandfather was a hooligan."

"You see, Nat, your Grandma Beverly insisted on coming with us to this underground card club. Once Charlie was losing, we tried to get him to leave, but he wouldn't. When he ran out of cash, he pulled a deed from his pocket and told us he was going to bet some land in Maine that had been left to him. I didn't want his family land falling into the hands of some gangster, so I bought my way into the game."

She watched her grandfather closely. "And that's when you won what became Woolwich Cove, right, Grandpa?"

"Yes," he answered with a solemn nod.

"But that's not all. Tell her, Hal?" her grandmother nudged.

Her grandfather sighed. "Charlie had gotten pretty drunk after losing everything. I don't think he remembers much after signing the deed over to me. We brought him home, and then your grandmother and I went back to the card club."

Natalie cocked her head to the side. "Why?"

"That's what I kept asking your grandfather on the drive

back over! I was livid! I thought he was going back to gamble."

Natalie searched her grandfather's eyes. "What did you go back for, Grandpa?"

"To pay Charlie's debts," the man answered.

Natalie sat back. "You're kidding?"

Grandpa Hal's cheeks grew the slightest bit pink. "Your grandmother wasn't wrong. I was a bit of a hooligan and a card shark in my day. So, I had the money."

"But that was all your grandfather's money—every last cent. And I knew the minute that he went back to that club and paid off Charlie's debt that he was the kind of man I could spend my life with," her grandmother answered.

"And then there was all the kissing," her grandfather added, causing her grandmother to blush, and the twist of a grin pulled at the corners of her grandfather's mouth. "And it wasn't all my money. We found a crinkled one-hundred-dollar bill in the glove box of my old Chevy. That's what I used to pay for your grandmother's ring, and then, we spent the money we had left on the hotel room we stayed in for our wedding night when we—"

Nat closed her eyes and shook her head. "Fast-forward through that part, please," she blurted, not ready to picture her grandparents like that when a question popped into her head. "And what did Charlie do when he learned you got married?"

Her grandmother Bev's expression grew serious. "My sister told me that when Charlie found out I'd married Hal, he packed up that day and moved out west."

Natalie glanced between them. "You didn't tell him that you'd paid off the gangsters?"

Hal sat back and steepled his fingers. "I have a feeling

Charlie knows what I did, but I didn't need to rub it in his face."

Natalie's thoughts spiraled. "Did you ever consider giving the land back?"

Her grandparents shared a serious look, and Grandpa Hal nodded.

"We'd considered it. But when we got here, I knew we'd done the right thing by keeping it. When Charlie looked at this land, he only saw dollar signs. But the moment we arrived and stared out at the ocean, we knew this place was special. We knew we were meant to be stewards of this land and do our best to share the beauty of this perfect slice of Maine with as many deserving people as possible."

Natalie stared out the window toward the ocean and imagined her grandparents, young and wild and free, staring out at the sea and promising to make a life together.

Her grandfather patted her cheek. "Here's the thing. Life is like the tides. The tide comes in, and the tide goes out. All you can do is accept what it brings and go from there."

"Did you really consider selling?" she asked as her gaze lingered on the sparkling water.

"What we considered was who would be the best choice to take over. So, we invited everyone here then stepped back, and with Fish's help, we were able to see what happened when someone needed to step up," her grandfather answered with a sly grin.

Natalie's hand flew to her chest. "You invited all the community groups to show up at the same time."

"And only two people came forward and made sure that everything ran smoothly," her grandmother replied.

"And those two people were you and Jake," her grandfather finished.

Bev gave her a knowing smile. "When your grandfather

and I first got here, we knew that our lives were meant to intersect. We had an instant connection to each other and to this place. You and Jake share that, too."

Nat closed her eyes and pressed her fingertips to her eyelids. "How do you know that Jake didn't do everything to try to trick us into selling? How do you know he wasn't pretending?"

"People who are pretending don't look at each other the way he looks at you and the way you look at him," her grandmother replied.

She sighed, and her gaze drifted back to the ocean. "Did he leave?"

"He did. Fish drove him into town," her grandfather answered.

"Not to the airport?" she replied, hating herself for the thread of hope that wove its way through her heart at the notion that Jake could still be nearby.

Grandma Bev patted her hand. "We don't know where he went from there, dear."

She nodded. "And the camp? Do you still trust me to run it on my own?"

Her grandfather glanced at his watch, then gestured to the door. "Let's take a walk. We still have a couple of hours until we're expected on Woolwich Island."

"For your vow renewal ceremony! That's tonight! You probably need to go, and I should get ready." Natalie sprang to her feet, then caught her reflection in the window. "Yikes, I need a shower."

"We've got time. Walk with us, Nat. We'd like to chat with you about what Camp Woolwich will look like moving forward," her grandfather said and gestured to the door.

Moving forward?

They left the lodge and took the trail that led to the cottages.

Her Grandpa Hal clasped his hands behind his back. "We'd like to set up a board of trustees. Your grandmother and I would serve in an advisory capacity only. All the decisions would be yours, but we also wanted to involve the community and invite some family members to participate as well."

"Your grandfather and I have already spoken to—"

"Grandpa, why did you want me to meet you here?" Leslie said, rounding the bend and cutting off their conversation.

"Perfect timing, dear," her grandmother said and squeezed her cousin's hand.

Heat rose to Natalie's cheeks. "Don't tell me you want Leslie on the board?"

"Why shouldn't I be on the board?" Leslie asked, giving her a healthy dose of side-eye.

Hal crossed his arms. "You girls have been butting heads for years, and for the sake of the camp, it's time that ended."

"Natalie, we want you to run the camp, but we'd like to have Leslie on the board, too," her grandmother added.

Natalie's gaze bounced between her grandparents. "But Leslie hates this place."

"I do not hate it," her cousin shot back.

Natalie released a heavy sigh. "Well, you hate me."

Leslie shrugged.

"All that ends today," her grandmother said with a little clap of her hands. "You're going to race each other and end this hostility once and for all."

"Race?" she and her cousin replied in unison.

"A tree-climbing race," her grandfather said, clearly suppressing a grin.

Leslie scoffed. "Are you serious?"

"Oh, yes. Like it or not, you both care about Camp Woolwich, and we want you both involved in its future. A good healthy race will help quash this competition between the two of you. Plus, we also need someone to clean the boys' latrine," her grandmother answered.

"What?" the women again echoed in unison.

"Yes, I told the boys that one of you would take care of it today," Hal added, not even trying to hide his amusement now.

"So, this is some kind of team building rah-rah thing, and the loser has to clean the boys' latrine?" Leslie clarified.

"Everyone has to contribute their part at Camp Woolwich. You both know that," her grandmother answered with a devious smile.

"That tree?" Leslie asked, gesturing with her chin.

Natalie stared up at the majestic oak, and a rush of confidence flooded her system. This was one of her favorite trees to climb as a girl, and after all that had gone down, she was *D, O, N, E,* done with her elder cousin's *I'm-better-than-you* attitude.

"Yep, this is the one," her grandfather said, rocking back on his heels to stare up at the towering oak.

Natalie met Leslie's gaze as if this were some Wild West duel. The women remained still for a beat then two before Natalie kicked off her cowgirl boots and sprinted toward the tree.

"Not so fast!" Leslie called, jerking off her sensible shoes, and running up behind her.

Natalie grabbed the first branch and pulled herself up. "I don't know why you've always hated me, Leslie."

"Oh, that's simple," Les bit back, working her way alongside. "Your everyone's favorite and you've had it easy your entire life."

Natalie sprang to the next leafy limb. "Had it easy? Where would you get that?"

"For starters," Leslie replied, grasping the next branch over. "You're grandma and grandpa's favorite."

Natalie batted at a cluster of gnats. "That's not true."

"And, you're an artist like Grandma. Growing up, they always doted on you," Leslie threw back, battling her own gnat battalion.

Natalie turned to tell off her cousin and was met with a mouthful of leaves. She spit and pushed the rogue limb out of the way. "I was the youngest! Didn't you know I wanted to be with you and the big kids?"

Leslie broke a nail and cursed, then edged her way closer. "Well, I never got to think of just myself. I always had to make sure Lara was okay. Do you know how hard it was getting her ass through podiatry school? For Christ's sake, when we were teenagers and our high school did a fundraiser to help raise funds for endangered whales, Lara asked me what I thought the whales would like to spend the money on?"

Breathing hard, their faces inches apart with bark in their hair and smudges of dirt on their cheeks, the women stilled and stared at one another. Another standoff, but Natalie cracked first, unable to hold back a full-belly laugh.

"You're kidding," she said, gasping for breath.

Leslie shook her head. Then something extraordinary happened. Her cousin's resting bitch face—well, always bitch face—disappeared. A genuine smile replaced her usual scowl as tears of laughter streamed down her cheeks.

"Oh, that's not even the half of it. Lara won't drink Mountain Dew because she truly believes it's made from dew harvested from a mountain top. And she thinks it's yellow because animals have peed on it." Les shook her head, still laughing. "She's truly the dumbest smart person I've ever met."

Natalie raised her finger. "Wait, get this! When we were kids and went into town to get licorice, she told me not to eat the black pieces because she was totally convinced that they'd fallen on the candy factory floor," Natalie said as she and her cousin broke into another fit of laughter.

"I always wondered what the hell she was doing when I'd catch her washing licorice in the sink!" Leslie replied through a bout of giggles.

After a moment, they quieted, and Leslie scooched over to share the branch with her.

"I never hated you, Nat. Truthfully, I've always been jealous of you. You're the pretty one. The artistic one. You were free to explore your passion and become an artist. You walk into a room, and everyone lights up."

Natalie's eyebrows shot up to her hairline. "How can you be jealous of me? Leslie, you're a doctor. You've always been the one in charge who had it together. If anything, I wished I could be more like you." She stared down at their dangling bare feet and remembered the time growing up before Leslie started teasing her. A time when they'd climb trees together and stare down from their leafy perch. She tapped Leslie's foot with hers just like they used to do when they were younger. "Is everything okay with Leo? You guys seem a little tense."

Leslie released a slow breath. "Wondering how we couldn't account four hundred thousand dollars can do that to a marriage."

"Are you guys going to be all right?" Nat asked.

Leslie chuckled. "Believe it or not, Leo found a solution."

Nat cocked her head to the side. "Somebody wants all those cinnamon roll-scented shoe inserts?"

"Yeah, Sweden has an actual Cinnamon Roll Day in October. The organizers of a cinnamon roll festival said they'd buy them all to give away as prizes. Can you imagine?" Leslie gazed down at her wedding ring. "You know, Leo really is a good guy when he's not all foot obsessed. And you've got to give Leo a little slack. You do have nice feet, Nat. Your arches are to die for. That's my professional opinion," she added with a wink.

"Well, if you ever need a foot model to peddle pizza or lobster-scented inserts, I'm happy to help," she answered, extending her leg and wiggling her toes.

Her cousin shifted on the branch. "Nat, are you going to be okay after what happened with Jake? I still can't believe he's your kiss keeper."

Natalie swallowed past the lump in her throat and tried to ignore the twinge in her heart. "I guess now we know the Kiss Keeper Curse is real."

Leslie frowned. "What do you mean?"

"Jake didn't kiss me at the well. Night patrol came, and we ran back to the cabin. He kissed me there by the screen door."

"Wow! I guess Otis Wiscasset can hold a grudge," Les answered, wide-eyed.

"So, I'm going to put all my energy into the camp," she answered because that was all she could do now.

Leslie tapped her foot. "Nat, I don't want to upset you, but Leo saw Jake this morning."

Natalie nearly lost her balance. "Where?"

"In town. Leo went in to talk with Grandma and Grandpa's lawyer to get a document ready for the cinnamon roll people. They really want these inserts."

"Did Leo say how Jake looked?" she asked, her pulse kicking up at the mention of the man.

"He said that Jake asked about you."

Natalie blinked back tears. "Oh yeah?"

"Then he told Leo to stay the hell away from your feet," Leslie said with a sympathetic smile.

Natalie toyed with a leaf. "I thought he was going to be my last Jake. The right Jake."

"And Lara and Marcus thought cinnamon roll shoe inserts would be the next big thing. Shit happens," Leslie teased, but the warmth in her eyes said she was only trying to ease the pain.

Natalie reached out and squeezed her cousin's hand. "Thanks, Les," she said softly, grateful to have her cousin back.

"Shit does happen, and that's why we need someone to clean the latrine," came her grandfather's booming voice that gave them such a startle they nearly fell off their branch.

"Have you been listening the whole time?" Nat called down.

"We're your grandparents. We're entitled to eavesdrop! And we all need you to shake a leg. You need to be ready for the vow renewal on the island in less than two hours."

"And the latrine?" Leslie called as the women cringed.

"Two are better than one at getting a job done," her grandmother replied.

Natalie shrugged. "I'll get the sinks. You take the floor, and we can split the urinals?"

"Deal. And you can tell me all your ideas for when you take over Camp Woolwich," Les replied with her genuine smile in place.

Nat nodded as her cousin started down the tree. But

before she began her descent, she stared out at the ocean, and her grandfather's words echoed in her mind.

The tide comes in, and the tide goes out. All you can do is accept what it brings and go from there.

"What will you bring me?" she whispered to the water, then shook her head at the silly question and followed her cousin down to the ground.

12

"I'll take whatever's on tap."

Jake nodded to the bartender, then sat down on a worn barstool and cradled his head in his hands.

Why the hell was he still here in the middle of freaking nowhere Maine? He huffed a pathetic little laugh. What a stupid question! He was there because he had nothing to go back to in Denver. It wasn't like that city was ever his home. No place had felt like home for the last fifteen years until...

He let out a weary sigh as the bartender set a glass of amber ale in front of him. He slid a twenty to the man. "Keep the change," he said, staring into his beer as if waiting for a message, telling him what the hell he was supposed to do now.

The last two days had been pure hell. After his heart had disintegrated inside his chest, watching Natalie sail away, he'd run into Charlie, who'd been waiting for him by the lodge.

The man tore into him—every which way.

You're through.

Your reputation is shit.

You can forget making the big money, you, pathetic orphan.

But like the summer rain, the man's words trailed down his cheeks and disappeared into the dirt. He didn't give a shit about Linton Holdings or, as Charlie put it, the chance of a lifetime he'd just pissed away. No, the only thought in his mind at that point was why.

Why hadn't he come clean to Natalie?

Why didn't he tell Hal and Bev that a developer was scheming to get their land?

What did he think was going to happen? Could he believe that Charlie would slink away or forget about Woolwich Cove? His phone blowing up with texts from the man should have clued him in on the fact that this was no ordinary property acquisition. But he'd been too busy pretending to be the Jake Natalie deserved. The agonizing catch was that the kind of man Natalie deserved wouldn't have used her in the first place. But that didn't change his broken heart, and it didn't suppress the ache in his limbs, sleeping without her in his arms the last two nights.

Christ! What he wouldn't give to hold her, kiss her, lose himself in the slide of their bodies, and the endless pools of green in her ocean eyes.

The door to the tavern opened, and the bartender, hunched over his phone, shot up as if he'd been summoned for active duty.

"Look at this, Dominic. It's the Garden of Eden cowboy I was telling you about."

Now it was Jake's turn to come to attention. "Sister Evangeline?"

"Well, it ain't the Pope," the nun answered with a sly expression, hoisting herself onto the barstool next to him as a young man set two helmets and a keyring on the counter.

"Hello, Sister," the bartender stuttered. "Is Sister Anne with you?"

"No, I'm here with Dominic today, and I'd like my gin martini," the woman answered, smoothing out her habit.

The bartender winced. "But Sister Anne said—"

The nun raised a wrinkled hand. "If Jesus can turn water into wine, an old nun can sneak off to enjoy a nip of gin, don't you agree?" She narrowed her gaze. "And it's been quite a while since we've seen you at mass, Trevor."

The bartender shifted his weight from foot to foot. "Yeah, sorry, Sister. I—"

"Am too busy fixing Sister Evangeline's martini," the nun supplied with the twist of a grin.

The bartender nodded and went to work, mixing the drink, and the nun swiveled in her seat.

"Jake, this handsome gentleman is Dominic. He's our gardener over at the convent," she said, gesturing over her shoulder.

The young man nodded to him, then turned to the nun. "All right, Sister, one drink while I run a few errands for Sister Anne, and no funny business, like the last time."

Jake raised an eyebrow. "What did she do last time?"

"She signed the convent up for Netflix," the gardener answered.

Sister Evangeline threw up her hands. "You can only pray for so many hours a day."

"Be good," the man warned, but his easy smile said he was fond of the feisty gal.

"So, Jake, why are you moping in your beer?" she asked as the gardener left the bar.

He sighed. He couldn't lie to a nun. "I'm cursed, and I lost Natalie."

"Cursed?" the nun repeated.

He traced a bead of condensation down the side of his glass. "Yes, have you heard of the Kiss Keeper Curse?"

"That first kiss business with the well near Camp Woolwich?" she asked as Trevor carefully set a martini with three olives in front of her.

Jake took a sip of his beer. "Yep, that's the one. Fifteen years ago, Natalie and I were supposed to kiss at that well. But we didn't, and now, I'm here, and she's done with me."

Sister Evangeline popped an olive into her mouth. "You're not cursed."

He reared back. "How would you know?"

"Because of Otis and Muriel," she answered, plucking another olive off the martini pick.

"What about them?" he pressed.

The nun leaned in and waved him to come closer as a sly grin pulled at the corners of her mouth. "Muriel Boothe never got on that boat headed back to England."

Nose to nose with a nun, Jake gasped. "How do you know that?"

"Muriel and Otis ran away together, all the way to California. To keep up appearances, the Boothe family let everyone believe that she was back in England," she said, sitting back and popping an olive into her mouth.

He wasn't sure if she was messing with him or not. He crossed his arms. "What proof do you have? It was ages ago."

"My great-great-grandmother was Muriel's cousin. They wrote to each other for many years. Muriel and Otis lived well into their eighties and had three daughters. The letters have been passed down in my family."

"Who has them now?" he asked.

"I do," she said with a demure sip of her drink.

Flabbergasted, his jaw dropped. "You do? Does anyone else know this?"

The nun shook her head. "I don't think so. It was just by luck that I was sent to Maine to teach in the parochial school in Portland," she answered casually as if she hadn't changed the course of Camp Woolwich history.

He ran his hands through his hair. "Why haven't you told anyone?"

Sister Evangeline lifted the martini to her lips, took another sip, then met his gaze over the rim of the glass. "People like legends, Jake. Stories bind people together. They weave their way into our communities, our minds, and our hearts."

"But it's not real?" he shot back incredulously.

The nun narrowed her gaze. "Does knowing that the legend isn't real lessen your connection to Natalie?"

A lump formed in his throat. "No, it doesn't."

"And even if this curse were real, everyone knows that true love can undo any otherworldly enchantment. Watch any old Disney movie," she added with a wink.

"You're right," he replied.

Sister Evangeline shrugged. "There you go."

But it wasn't just a curse that he had to defeat.

He slumped forward. "But she hates me. I deceived her. Even if the curse is bogus, how can I account for my behavior? How can I ever be worthy of her?"

The nun nodded solemnly. "Let me ask you this. What would you do if, magically, all your guilt, shame, and self-doubt disappeared?"

He sat back as the image of Natalie, gazing up at him in line at the airport, flashed through his mind. Even then, she'd had his heart.

"I'd do whatever it takes to get to her. I'd tell her that the only thing I want in this world is to spend the rest of my life proving myself to her, showing her how much she means to me, and how much Camp Woolwich means to me," he replied, surprised at how easy it was to spill his guts to the feisty nun.

Sister Evangeline's expression grew serious. She closed her eyes, then raised her hand and snapped her fingers, startling him and almost knocking him off the damn stool.

"Okay, it's done," she said and took another sip of her martini.

"What's done?" he asked, his gaze bouncing from the nun to the bartender who shrugged his confusion.

"I checked in with the big guy upstairs. You're forgiven," she said, gesturing for Trevor to bring her a bowl of olives.

"I am? You can do that?" Jake stammered, glancing around, looking for a ray of light or possibly a thunderbolt. Something that spoke of divine intervention.

"I'm a nun," she answered with a wave of her hand.

"Can she do that?" he asked Trevor.

"She sure gets her way a lot. I'll give her that," the guy replied.

The woman chuckled then stilled.

"What is it? Are you getting another message?" Jake asked, checking for a cherub or a burning bush.

Shit! He'd wished he'd paid attention in Sunday school.

"It doesn't work like that," she said, then handed him a helmet and swiped the keys from the counter.

He frowned. "What are you doing?"

"God's work," she said, placing the large helmet on her little nun head.

"Which is?" he questioned.

"Love," she offered.

"Love," he repeated.

The nun watched him closely. "You love Natalie, right?"

"Yes," he replied as the weight of his predicament sank in.

He loved her. This girl who'd lived in his heart since he was a boy. This blindfolded beauty who'd been a beacon of light in his darkest days. She was that kernel of hope that remained even after the heartbreak of losing his parents and the misery of growing up on his uncle's dairy farm. He may have lost his way in this world and constructed a life that was nothing more than a house of cards built on deals and dollars, but that wasn't who he was. During this time with Natalie, the hope in his heart had reignited, the lessons he'd learned from his parents had been reborn, and he'd experienced the pure, real joy of loving another.

The nun snapped again, jolting him from his thoughts.

"Hey, loverboy! Pay for my drink, then meet me outside," she said, hopping off the stool.

Still reeling, he shifted the helmet under his arm and pulled out his wallet and placed a fifty on the bar.

The bartender shook his head and slid back the bill. "No worries, man. It's always on the house for the sisters."

"But I feel like you've earned this," he said with the hint of a grin.

The bartender dropped the bill into the tip jar. "Thanks, and good luck with your girl."

He nodded to the man. Curse or no curse, he needed all the luck and divine intervention he could get. He stepped out onto the sidewalk, ready to find Natalie when he found Sister Evangeline sitting atop a motorcycle with an attached sidecar.

"What's all this, Sister?" he asked.

"I told you, God's work," she answered with a deceptively sweet smile.

He cocked his head to the side. "God's work is riding a motorcycle?"

"No, you idiot," she said with an annoyed shake of her head. "God's work is borrowing Dominic's bike to take you to Camp Woolwich to find Natalie."

His brow creased. "You can drive that thing?"

Like a tiny nun ninja, she kick-started the old bike and revved the engine.

"Holy—" he began, but Sister Evangeline pinned him with her gaze.

"Cow," he substituted for holy fucking crazy shit! Because that's what this was.

"Get in," she called over the grumble of the engine.

He paced the sidewalk. This is what he wanted, right? A chance to get her back. The opportunity to show her that he loved her and that he wanted to make a life with her. He stared at his reflection in the window of the shop next to the bar when a sparkle caught his eye.

A ring.

He pressed his hands to the glass to find a Natalie green emerald, right there, staring up at him as if the universe had planted it.

"Give me a second," he called to the nun, then ran inside, and, in less than five minutes, he'd purchased a...what?

An engagement ring?

He stared down at the sparkling gem. "Sister, do you have a phone?" he called over the engine's sputtering purr.

The woman reached into a pocket and handed him her cell. "Don't let Sister Anne know I have this."

He mimicked zipping his lips, then clicked on the web browser, and searched for Camp Woolwich. When the page came up, he saw the button he needed, completed the transaction, then handed the phone back to Sister Evangeline.

"You didn't cancel my Netflix subscription, did you?" she asked.

"No, I pledged to donate ten million dollars to Camp Woolwich," he said, tucking the ring box into his pocket, then put on his helmet.

The nun's jaw dropped as he maneuvered his massive body into the snug sidecar, grinning like the happiest guy on earth because he was.

He was all in. All that money would be hers, just like his heart. Even if she were to kick him to the curb, he wanted the camp to have it. With or without him, that money would provide the funds for generation after generation of campers.

He glanced at the nun. "Are you sure you're okay to drive after that martini?"

The woman scoffed. "You think one martini does anything for me. I could drink you under the table every day of the week and twice on Sunday," she called, looking half her age with a wide, girlish grin.

He didn't doubt it.

The nun revved the bike, and they were off, speeding down Main Street. The shops and restaurants thinned out as the motorcycle zoomed down the highway toward Camp Woolwich. He relaxed into the snug space and allowed his thoughts to drift. Memories of his mother and father, once locked away in his heart, came flooding back, washing over him like the tranquil coastal breeze.

Sailing trips on the lake, tying knots with his father, and nights spent in their little boat's cabin, playing board games and laughing, danced in his memory and warmed his heart.

Those years had been jam-packed with so much laughter and such profound joy.

He'd tried to forget, fearing that the pain of never experiencing real happiness again would be worse than the stoic numbness he'd forced himself to adopt. But loving Natalie had cracked open his hardened heart.

No matter what happened next, his life would be different.

He would be different.

He'd choose kindness over cash flow and sincerity over sales.

He would do better. Be better.

"I could use your help getting her back," he whispered to his parents as a warmth filled his chest, but he didn't have long to dwell on the sensation as the Camp Woolwich sign came into view.

The old motorcycle turned onto the camp's bumpy road as they entered the property then passed the parking area near the lodge.

"Where are you going?" he called to the nun.

She maneuvered the bike onto the path that led to the waterfront, and then he remembered.

The vow renewal ceremony was tonight on Woolwich Island.

Across the cove.

Separated from the mainland by a narrow stretch of the ocean.

An island only accessible by boat.

"There's one left," the woman called, cutting the engine.

He took off his helmet. "One what?"

"Sailboat. The family's gone to their island for the vow renewal. Bev told us about their plans that day we came for our art class. You know, the day where you wouldn't pose naked for us," she answered with a pout.

He stared at the boat. "I have to sail?"

"Unless you can walk on water," the nun countered.

He maneuvered his body out of the tiny sidecar and stretched his long limbs, staring out across the cove. In the hazy twilight, lights from the island twinkled, winking at him, calling to him.

"You know how to sail, don't you?" Sister Evangeline asked.

He nodded. "My parents taught me when I was a boy."

"Then what's stopping you?" she challenged.

Nothing.

The fear and sorrow in his heart made way for an ocean of love. He rigged the little boat, securing the lines and hoisting the mast just as his parents had taught him to do on Lake Michigan.

"I owe you, Sister," he called, catching the wind as the boat glided away from the dock onto the shimmering sea.

"Well, you haven't gotten her back yet," the woman replied, but her wide grin let him know she was pulling for him.

And speaking of pulling, he needed to get his head in the game. As if his parents were right there with him in that little Sunfish, he pulled in the flapping sail. He hadn't done this in over a decade, but it all came back to him. The rock of the boat. The feel of the line in one hand and the tiller in the other. He could almost see his father pointing, showing him how to pick a point in the distance, and he set a course for the little island with its beachfront littered with canoes, kayaks, and sailboats tethered to a weathered dock.

A peace settled over him. The same calmness he remembered, listening to his parents' voices lull him to sleep on their overnight boat trips. That is, until the little boat glided in next to the dock, and he realized he hadn't made a plan. In fact, he was flying by the seat of his pants.

What the hell was he going to say to the woman he loved?

Where should he start, and what would her family do to him? He, the guy who initially was there to get their land, then pretty much duped the beloved Woolwich grand-daughter, and broke her heart in the process, had stolen a Camp Woolwich sailboat and sailed to Woolwich Island to crash a vow renewal.

He, the slick guy with a scheme for everything, had no strategy, but when he felt the corner of the tiny box in his pocket dig into his thigh, a sense of euphoria rushed through him.

He had a ring.

He patted the outline of the small box. "Here we go. Wish me luck," he whispered to his parents.

The sound of violins carried on the breeze, and he sprinted up a sandy trail toward the glowing lights coming from the center of the island. Brush had been trimmed back, but the place still had a wild, uninhabited feel. He worked his way through the winding path, picking up speed until he caught his toe on a tree root and pitched forward.

"Shit!" he cried, stumbling to get his balance when the violin music came to a squeaky, screeching halt, and he looked up to find a large covered gazebo with twinkling lights and row upon row of seated Woolwiches, all staring at him.

Like a wild animal, he scanned their faces, searching for Natalie. Hal and Bev stood along with an officiant at the far end of the gazebo with their heads cocked to the side. No one spoke a word as he continued to survey the group when a hand grabbed his arm.

"What are you doing here? How did you even get here?" Natalie demanded in a harsh whisper.

"I sailed over?" he whispered back.

She frowned. "You stole a boat and sailed here by yourself?"

"Yeah, because I need to tell you something," he whispered back, then looked over to find that all eyes were on them.

She crossed her arms. "Well?"

He leaned in so only she could hear. "Muriel never got on the boat."

She reared back. "What are you talking about?"

"Muriel Boothe, the girl Otis Wiscasset loved," he said, keeping his voice down.

Natalie's brows knit together. "Yes? What about her?"

"She never got on the boat back to England. She and Otis ran off to California. They lived a long life together and had kids and everything," he whispered, his gaze bouncing between Natalie and the many, many sets of unfriendly Woolwich gazes.

Curiosity edged out anger in Natalie's expression. "How do you know that?"

Good. At least, she was talking to him.

"I was drinking with that horny nun in town, and she told me the real story of Otis and Muriel. Then she drove me back to camp in the sidecar of her gardener's motorcycle, so I could find you and tell you that there's no curse," he replied as her angry expression returned.

"How much have you had to drink, Jake Teller, because you sound insane. And if you're here out of some misplaced sense of duty, you can get back on the stolen boat and leave.

I don't need you or your help. I'm taking over the camp myself. I'm never letting this land leave my family, and I'm not afraid to do this on my own," she answered, raising her voice for all to hear.

He took her hands into his. "I'm not insane. Okay, maybe I am, but it's only because I cannot lose you, Natalie. I never thought I'd sail again, but the thought of not spending the rest of my life here with you was the kick in the ass I needed to make me confront my fears and let go of the past and focus on what really matters. That's you and Camp Woolwich. I know you could run the camp without me. But I hope that in your heart, you know that you don't have to."

She stared past him, shaking her head as her eyes welled with tears, but she didn't pull away.

He glanced at the Woolwich clan, who were still watching, then exhaled a slow breath. He had to lay it all on the line. It was now or never.

He swallowed hard. "Maybe you and I started out as a con, but I'm pretty sure we both knew the minute that we met that we were meant to be together. I tried to deny it, but my heart knew. And your heart knows this, too."

Her eyes shined as she held back tears. "Jake, I don't know if I can trust you."

He cupped her face in his hand and held her gaze. "Heels, I thought that making lots of money would fill the void inside me. I thought that it would give me complete control over my life. I never wanted to depend on anyone the way I was forced to depend on my uncle. But it never worked. There was never enough until I met you. Well, met you for the second time, and you brought me back to Camp Woolwich. You helped me remember the kind of person I want to be and the kind of person who my parents would be proud of. The kind of person who gives back and the kind of man who gives his whole heart to the woman he loves."

"You love me?" she gasped.

He nodded. "Yes, more than anything in this world."

She glanced away. "But what about all my failed relationships with the wrong Jakes? Why would you be any different?"

Dammit, she had a point. A lot of Jakes had let her down.

"What if he's the right Jake?" Hal called from across the gazebo.

"And remember, none of us are perfect. Mistakes are part of the process, dear," Natalie's grandmother added.

He looked to the couple, profoundly grateful to have them rooting for him, then turned to Natalie. In his past life, this would have been the part where he'd close the deal. He'd bullshit his way to get everything the way he wanted it. But tonight, he didn't have to bullshit. He had love on his side. That emotion he'd once dubbed as something only for the weak had become his fountain of strength.

"Maybe all those Jakes made up a dating roadmap, leading you to the right Jake. The Jake who wants every part of you. Because if you'll take me, Natalie, I want to be your last Jake and your kiss keeper every day for the rest of our lives." He steadied himself and stared into her emerald ocean eyes. "We shared our first kiss. Let me keep all your kisses from here on out. I love you, Natalie Callahan. I've loved you since I was thirteen years old, and I will never stop."

"Oh, Jake," she rasped as a tear trailed down her cheek.

He brushed it away and smiled through his tears. "And, there's more."

"More?" she exclaimed.

He nodded. "No matter what you decide. If you allow me to stay or tell me to go, the money is yours."

"What money?" she asked.

A Woolwich teen held up his phone. "Somebody pledged ten million big ones to the camp. It's right here on the website!"

He brushed another tear from her cheek. "It's the best investment I've ever made."

"Ten million dollars?" she repeated with wide eyes.

"That could buy a lot of cinnamon roll-scented foot inserts."

He and Natalie glanced over at the Woolwich pack to find Lara and Marcus nodding and whispering to each other before Leslie cupped her hand over her sister's mouth.

"Foot inserts?" he asked.

Natalie released a teary chuckle. "It's a long story."

"Well, that ten million is everything I have, and it's yours. With or without me, it's yours," he added softly.

She smiled up at him. "Today, before we left for the island, I asked the tide what it was going to bring me, and now, you're here."

His pulse kicked up. She wasn't telling him to leave.

"We're not cursed, Natalie. And even if we were, I don't feel cursed when I hold you in my arms. All I feel is complete."

"Me, too," she answered.

"I'm sorry I didn't tell you about what Charlie wanted me to do," he said, his voice shaking.

She wiped a tear from his cheek. "I know you are."

"Can you forgive me, Heels?"

There it was, the question that held all the weight.

She watched him, staring into his eyes. "You heard what

my grandmother said about mistakes. We're good at second chances here at Camp Woolwich."

He rested his forehead against hers. "Say you'll be mine, Heels. Tell me that I can help you carry on your family's legacy. Say we'll be each other's kiss keeper forever."

"I've always been yours. It just took six Jakes to get to you," she answered with a teary, teasing grin as a chorus of cheers broke out, but the applause abruptly stopped when he stepped back and took a knee.

"Jake, what's that?" she asked, staring at the box in his hand.

He glanced at the sparkling ring. "We've only known each other a week, and it might seem crazy to do this after such a short time, but when I saw this ring today, I knew it was the ring I was meant to give to you when I asked you to be my wife."

"A week isn't that short," Hal called from underneath a garland of wildflowers.

"And, it's seven times longer than I knew her grandfather before I married him," Bev added.

"What's that all about?" he asked.

She grinned. "It's another long story. I'll tell you about it later."

"We get to have a later?" he asked.

Her eyes sparkled. "Yes, but you should probably hurry up this proposal. We are kind of hijacking my grandparents' vow renewal."

He chuckled and then blew out a shaky breath. "Natalie Callahan, you've had my heart since I was thirteen years old, and you always will. And if you'll have me, I will love you every day, and I will keep your kisses every night. Will you be my wife?"

"Aunt Nat and Uncle Jake should get married now!" Annabelle called.

"Yeah! Up with Mimi and Poppy," Josie and Maddy chimed.

Hal gestured to the altar. "There's plenty of room up here."

"What do you say? Should we close this deal?" Natalie asked with a sly wink.

With his parents and, he suspected, the ghosts of Muriel Boothe and Otis Wiscasset smiling down on them, he slid the ring onto her finger, then gazed into her ocean eyes.

"Lead the way, Heels."

EPILOGUE
JAKE

"I think I understand why podiatrists can barely control themselves around your feet, Heels. You do have damn perfect arches," he growled, holding his wife's ankle as he pressed a kiss to her perfect foot.

"Do I have to add you to my foot pervert list?" Natalie teased with a sweet sigh.

"Oh, no. As your husband, I'm tasked with being your foot protector," he replied.

With her hair fanned out on the pillow and her hands gripping the iron rods of the bed's headboard, Natalie captured his gaze with hungry eyes. "And, as my husband, you're also tasked with another very important job, and it's got nothing to do with my feet."

"Your knees?" he teased, pressing a kiss to each.

"You're getting warmer," she purred.

"This freckle on your thigh?" he asked, trailing his tongue farther up her leg.

"Even warmer," she answered on a dreamy moan.

"How about here?" he asked and began rubbing tiny circles to her most sensitive place.

"Hot," she breathed as he worked her with his hand and watched her naked body writhe beneath his touch.

Growing slick with desire, she rocked against him, and a fiery jolt of lust went straight to his cock. He'd never tire of this view. And, thanks to the help of a horny nun and a fake curse that turned out to be a real blessing, he'd never have to.

The moment after Natalie Callahan became his wife, in true Jake Teller form, he'd thrown her over his shoulder and high-tailed it back to the little Sunfish where he'd sailed them back to camp, then carried her all the way to their cottage. And that's where they'd stayed for three days in a gloriously sweaty, orgasmic haze.

They were smart to take that time because once they emerged, life moved fast.

Hal and Bev had turned Camp Woolwich over to them, but he'd made damn sure that Natalie was the sole owner. Not because he didn't trust himself, but because he did. He trusted that the life he was going to build with her was the kind of life that could weather any storm.

He didn't need property or millions of his own. He'd gained the security and love he'd craved when he gave his heart to his kiss keeper.

And as far as the Kiss Keeper Curse, they'd decided to preserve Otis and Muriel's secret and keep the Camp Woolwich legend intact. Sister Evangeline had shared Muriel's letters with them. Crinkled and worn, the old ink spelled out how Muriel and Otis did have their first kiss at the well before heading out west to make a life together. A life that in Muriel's words spoke of a fair share of hardships, but also great love and an abundance of joy. And the lesson that, whatever fate brings, always hold tight to the ones you love.

A lesson they'd already put into practice.

A year had blown by in the blink of an eye, and tonight was the last night of summer camp. In the morning, the campers' families would arrive to load up the trunks and box away the memories of a summer spent on Woolwich Cove.

With his business knowledge and Natalie's organizational skills and artistic eye, the summer had gone off without a hitch, and life was good. Damn good.

"Jake, I want to feel you," she whispered on a tight breath, teetering on the edge.

Music to his ears.

He positioned himself at her entrance, then kissed his way up her neck to her lips. He captured her mouth, and their tongues met in a sensual kiss as he drove inside her. He palmed her ass with one hand while the other wrapped around her wrists, making love to her in deep, wantonness thrusts. Their mingled breaths grew ragged as the friction between them ignited into an inferno of desire.

All summer, their mornings, afternoons, and evenings had belonged to the camp. But once lights-out hit, Natalie was his, and he'd savored every moment.

She wrapped her legs around him and pressed her perfect heels into his ass, allowing him to go deeper and harder—just the way his wife liked it.

"Jake, I'm so close," she breathed, meeting him blow for blow as their bodies came together.

Heat and sweat building between them, they soared higher and higher until, with a primal cry, he drove them over ecstasy's edge. True to his promise, he kept her kisses, devouring them, one after another, after another as they greedily drew pleasure from the slap and grind of their bodies.

Natalie hummed a sweet sigh beneath him, slowly

coming back from the bliss of release. He pressed up onto his elbows, then brushed a lock of hair from her face and frowned.

"What is it?" she asked lazily.

"You've still got a little green face paint on your cheek," he said, staring down at her beautiful face.

She pursed her lips. "That's your fault."

"My fault?" he asked with a cheeky grin.

She traced the shell of his ear with her fingertip. "You were the one with the idea for Alien Night."

He slid his hand to her shoulder and brushed his thumb back and forth, across her collarbone. "Okay, maybe the face paint turned out to be a fiasco, but the laser light show was worth it."

While they weren't about to start spending the money he'd donated recklessly, Natalie had allowed him to purchase a planetarium-grade laser light show machine, which was freaking awesome.

She traced her fingertips across the scruff on his cheek. "Yes, the kids loved it."

He pressed a kiss to the corner of her mouth. "What are your thoughts on getting one of those ninja warrior giant rectangle things?"

"For the kids or for you?" she asked with a sly smile when her phone began to chime.

"What's that for?" he asked.

"Oh, I forgot to tell you. I told the counselors scheduled for tonight's night patrol that you and I would take it, being that it's the last night of camp," she answered, playing with the hair at the nape of his neck.

"Are you telling me that we have to leave this bed?" he asked, pinning her with his gaze.

She gave him a naughty little smile. "I'm telling you that

we get to take a night stroll around the camp and then over to the—"

"Kiss Keeper's well," he finished, meeting her naughty little grin with one of his own.

"Yes, and maybe for a late-night skinny-dip over by the abandoned lighthouse," she added.

He kissed her neck and inhaled her sweet scent. "You've really thought about this, Mrs. Teller."

"It is the last night of camp," she tossed back.

"And the anniversary of our first kiss," he answered, remembering the blindfolded mystery girl, standing in the moonlight.

They dressed quickly, and he pulled on his cap as they left the main house. It was easier living there, in the center of camp, than staying in their little cottage. And thank God, they had the place to themselves. Hal's health had improved, and he and Bev had left for a cruise around the world right before camp started. But to be on the safe side, he and Natalie had hired an architect to draw up plans for a cozy one-story bungalow right on the water, which would allow the Woolwich camp founders to relax, but also be close enough to enjoy camp life—when they wanted.

He grabbed the flashlight next to the door and took Natalie's hand as they fell into step and started the loop. He didn't mind night patrol. With his wife by his side and the ocean's quiet, rhythmic lullaby woven in with the buzz of the woods at night, it was hard to think of anyplace he loved more.

They rounded the curve and headed toward the well when Natalie stopped and squeezed his hand.

"Jake, look. I think it's Finn," she whispered as two blind-folded forms awkwardly approached the well.

He led her behind a wall of spruce pines, and Natalie

leaned into him as they peeked out through the needles, watching the nervous teens. He rested his hand on her shoulder, and, like he'd done that first night and probably a hundred times since they'd reconnected, he brushed his thumb across her collarbone.

"Looks like the Kiss Keeper legend lives on," she said, staring up at him with no blindfold between them.

"And it always will," he replied, then leaned in and pressed his lips to hers, offering up another kiss.

I hope you enjoyed The Kiss Keeper. While this is a standalone story, I'd love to invite you to start reading my rom-com Man Fast. It's the first book in the Bergen Brothers Series, featuring three billionaire brothers and three feisty heroines ready to bring these handsome men to their knees. If you enjoyed The Kiss Keeper, you'll love the Bergen Brothers. Get ready to laugh, sigh, and swoon!

THE INSIDE SCOOP
THE KISS KEEPER

The time spent at a summer camp on the East Coast are my favorite teenage memories. I always wanted to write a story that wove this time of my life into a work of fiction, and when I created Natalie and Jake, I knew that they were the right couple to send to camp.

I love all the firsts I experienced at camp. First kiss. First time out on sailboat. First time sneaking out to meet boys. First time away from home for weeks on end.

If you can't tell, I adored everything about it. Almost thirty years later, all I have to do is close my eyes, and I can feel the ocean air coming off the water and kissing my cheeks.

Sign up for Krista's newsletter to stay in the loop and get new release announcements delivered right to your in-box.

BONUS: A LOVE LETTER FROM JAKE TO NATALIE

Dear Heels,

Yeah, I'm going to call you Heels instead of Natalie.

You know why.

We need to get a few things straight.

I'm not the Jake for you.

And let's address the *elephant,* I mean, *Jake-a-phant* in the room.

Six Jakes? You've dated six Jakes—in a row?

You'd think that after four or five let you down, you'd migrate to a couple Steves or even a Gary or two.

I've got news for you.

I won't be number seven—at least, that's what I'm telling myself.

I'm a lone wolf, but you gave me no choice when you barreled into my life, wearing that sexy as hell trench coat and, yes, those damned red high heels.

Sweet Jesus!

Here's the thing.

I don't get involved with women. I'm not the one to call

when a freight train is on a collision course with some damsel in distress tied to the tracks.

I'm a ruthless businessman.

I'm in it for the kill.

The win.

The cold hard cash.

I've got the body of a Greek god. I don't need to chase women.

Well, I didn't...

Until you.

It was as if the universe had put a plan in motion—an elaborate meet-cute that wasn't exactly our first meet-cute.

From the first time I met your gaze, I was a goner.

Those sea-green eyes, harkening back to the ebb and flow of the ocean, the twist of rope in my hand as I sailed with the wind at my back and a future of unlimited possibilities ahead of me.

That's how life would have worked out if life were a fairy tale.

But you and I know that life can throw one hell of a sucker punch and tangle you in its web.

That's where we are, Heels. You and me. Tangled together.

You don't even realize the extent of our web.

I should do what I have to do and get out.

My life is transactional.

Money. Sex. Power. Once the deal is done, I'm gone.

Except with you.

I keep finding reasons to stay...with you.

And why can't I keep my damned hands off you?

My icy demeanor melts at your touch.

This thing between us isn't supposed to be real.

We agreed to play our parts and keep up our little scheme.

And this con you're trying to run—this attempt to convince your family that you've got your shit together?

I don't get it.

Your family is nuts!

I shouldn't say that your entire family is a few fries short of a happy meal. Your grandparents are great, and those tree-climbing nieces and nephews of yours are pretty cute— if cute kids were my thing.

They're not.

Nope, not even when I'm rescuing them from a high tree branch or fishing with them or watching them shovel oatmeal into their adorable mouths.

Nope, kids are totally not my thing.

But I digress. When I said your family was fucking nuts, I meant the Dix Foot Freaks.

Sorry! It's only that their last name is *Dixtown*, and I couldn't help myself.

Try saying *Dixtown* three times fast without laughing your ass off.

Here's a hint...it's not going to happen.

Those cousins of yours and their podiatrist foot-obsessed husbands could give a screenwriter enough material to craft the creepiest of low budget, B level horror flicks.

But here we are, surrounded by those foot-loving freaks, at your grandparents' summer camp on the coast of Maine, playing the happy couple.

Moment of truth.

I'm not playing.

The minute your idiot cousins roped us into a game of truth or dare, I wanted them to dare us to kiss.

And when they did, the damn earth rocked off its axis.

Heels, those petal-soft lips of yours could bring a man to his knees.

Scratch that.

Those petal-soft lips of yours brought me to my knees.

And it didn't stop with the kiss.

Nope, we dove head-first into *intercourse*.

Yep, the *I word* that sounds like some dweeb in a lab coat who'd never gotten laid invented it.

Except when you say it, my cock is ready to grab a damned beaker and nerd out like an X-rated version of Bill Nye, the intercourse-loving science guy.

Christ! Have I lost myself, or have I found myself?

The truth is, Heels, you've had my heart for a long time —a lot longer than you could ever know.

The question is, will I ever be worthy of yours?

But you and I know that's not our choice to make.

That decision lies in the hands of the kiss keeper.

Yours in all things intercourse,

Jake (the seventh one)

ALSO BY KRISTA SANDOR

The Bergen Brothers Series

A sassy and sexy series about billionaire brothers.

Book One: Man Fast

Book Two: Man Feast

Book Three: Man Find

Bergen Brothers: The Complete Series+Bonus Short Story

Own the Eights Series

A delightfully sexy enemies to lovers series.

Book One: Own the Eights

Book Two: Own the Eights Gets Married

Book Three: Own the Eights Maybe Baby (Fall 2020)

The Langley Park Series

A steamy, suspenseful second-chance at love series.

Book One: The Road Home

Book Two: The Sound of Home

Book Three: The Beginning of Home

Book Four: The Measure of Home

Book Five: The Story of Home

Sign up for Krista's newsletter to stay in the loop and get new release announcements delivered right to your in-box.

ABOUT THE AUTHOR

KRISTA SANDOR

If there's one thing Krista Sandor knows for sure, it's that romance saved her.

After she was diagnosed with Multiple Sclerosis in 2015, her world turned upside down.

During those difficult first days, her dear friend sent her a romance novel. That kind gesture provided the escape she needed and ignited her love of the genre.

Inspired by the strong heroines and happily ever afters, Krista decided to write her own romance novels. Today, she is an MS Warrior and living life to the fullest. When she's not writing, you can find her running 5Ks with her handsome husband and chasing after her growing boys in Denver, Colorado.

Never miss a release, contest, or author event! Visit Krista's website www.KristaSandor.com and sign up to receive her exclusive newsletter.

ACKNOWLEDGMENTS

I have many to thank for helping me bring The Kiss Keeper to life.

Dear readers, reviewers, bloggers, bookstagrammers, and ARC readers, thank you for giving me and my books a shot. So many of you have become close friends. I give thanks every day for our loving and supportive romance community.

Tera, Kendra, and Marla, your careful edits and attention to all those grammar details make The Kiss Keeper sparkle and shine.

Candy Castle Crew, this cover is absolutely perfect! Thank you for your hard work!

Michelle Dare, my dear friend and mentor, thank you for your guidance. I thank the stars for you every day.

S.E. Rose, my BFF and writing partner in crime. I don't know what I'd do without you. You are a beacon of love and kindness. I can't wait for our next adventure.

David, my husband, and my best friend, thank you for supporting me every step of the way. I love you.

Made in the USA
Columbia, SC
01 July 2021